SEDUCTIVE HEARTS

ELITE HEIRS OF MANHATTAN BOOK 1

MISSY WALKER

Copyright © 2024 by Missy Walker

All rights reserved.

No part of this publication may be reproduced, distributed or transmitted in any form or by any means, including by any electronic or mechanical means, including photocopying, recording or information storage and retrieval systems, without prior written consent from the author, except for the use of brief quotations in a book review.

Cover Design: Missy Walker

Editor: Swish Design & Editing

To my daughters...
I hope you're lucky enough to find the person of your dreams.
Please, never settle. Life's too fucking short for mediocrity.

Elite *Men* Of Manhattan and Elite *Heirs* of Manhattan Family Tree

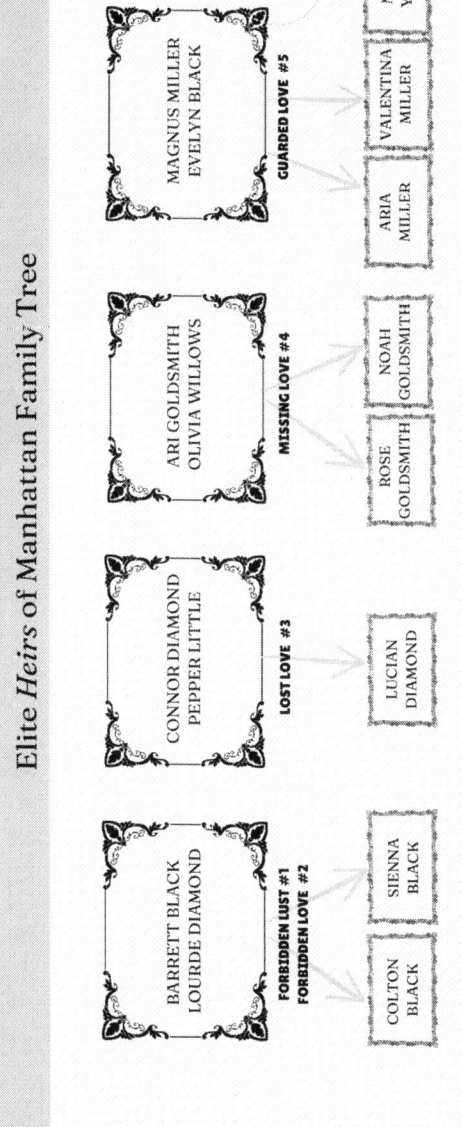

1

COLTON

Very few things could ruin a night out with my closest friends.

A text from my father was one of them. Bonus points if he was good and pissed.

Dad: *Get your ass home. Now. My study.*

He was definitely good and pissed. It didn't matter that I had a home of my own, nor that I was in the middle of having drinks with the guys. The great Barrett Black had made a proclamation and expected the world to comply.

I settled back in my chair, staring at the message while holding a glass of scotch in my other hand. "Fuck me," I muttered before finishing off the rest of my drink, savoring the heat which spread through my chest. It was a lot more pleasant than the burning, seething heat Dad's constant scrutiny usually stirred up in me.

"Fuck you? No, thanks." My cousin, Lucian Diamond, laughed before lifting his hand to get our server's attention—a cute girl but too perky for my taste, somebody who probably would never rub shoulders with people like us if it wasn't for her job. She knew it was in her best interest to smile brightly and be a little flirtatious, and she had given us plenty of both.

She flashed that blinding smile again when she joined us. Her gaze darted around the small corner table, taking us in one at a time—Lucian, Noah Goldsmith, one of my oldest friends, Evan, and me. Tipping her blonde head to the side, she asked, "Are you all brothers? I swear, you look so much alike!"

We did, somewhat—tall, dark-haired, athletic. Maybe the similarities appeared stronger in the bar's dim lighting, or perhaps she was kissing ass for a bigger tip by starting a conversation, getting personal. "Something like that," I settled for.

"Wow. What a gorgeous family." She shook her head like she couldn't believe it before asking, "What can I get you, boys?"

Noah had been my best friend practically since we were born, so it didn't come as a surprise when he leaned back in his chair and deliberately looked her up and down. "I don't know. Are *you* on the menu?" he asked before sharing the kind of grin that normally sent a woman's panties sliding to the floor.

"Don't listen to him." Evan shook his head and pretended to scowl at Noah. "He has no manners."

Lucian lifted his hand to regain the girl's attention. "I was going to order another round. How does that sound?" he asked, looking around the table.

"Not for me." I knew I would catch hell for it, but I refused the offer. "Gotta go take care of something."

"Or someone?" Evan asked, snickering once the server bounced away. He gazed at her retreating ass before grunting out, "Dibs on that one."

Noah knew me best and laughed knowingly. He narrowed his eyes, looking me up and down as I patted my pockets to make sure I had everything. "No, not the way you're thinking," he predicted with a snicker, elbowing Evan to get his attention. "I know that look."

Shooting him a cold glare, I demanded, "What look?"

"The look that says your balls crawled up into your belly when you got that text from Barrett," he announced with a laugh. "Sorry. I could see the screen from here." The others laughed with him, which was no big surprise, while I quietly seethed.

"Go fuck yourself," I grumbled once they calmed down. Certain topics were off-limits as far as I was concerned, at least in public—no busting each other's balls about our demanding parents.

And in my case, disappointed parents. No, *parent*. Singular. There wasn't much I could do or say that would get my mom too upset. The few times I'd ever witnessed my parents arguing was over me and the fact that Dad thought she was too easy on me. More than once, he'd called me a spoiled brat. All because he'd worked to get where he was, while all I'd ever had to do was rely on him and my trust. It's not my fault I wasn't driven like he was, not having goals and ambitions and all that shit.

"He can't know about Veronica yet, can he?" Lucian's brows knitted together before he winced. "I mean, unless he got word from my dad." He winced again, almost like he felt guilty for his father making a phone call.

Yes, trouble seemed to find me again this evening, but then again, Veronica never could handle her liquor. To think her wild temper was one of the things that had drawn me to her in the first place. That and a killer pair of legs that went up to her neck and tits with the power to make me drool. I couldn't keep my dick from waking up a little at the memory.

But not for the first time did I ask myself what the point was of having a media empire in the family if stories about a good-for-nothing playboy having a public blowout with an internationally famous model couldn't be suppressed.

Would that be too much to ask?

A little family loyalty?

No, instead, our dads lived by their ancient bro code. Uncle Connor would have rather gone behind my back and rat me out to my old man than bail me out for once.

"I'll deal with it, either way," I told him, then lifted a hand before leaving the table and making my way to the exit. The bar was pretty damn close to packed, full of beautiful bodies, some of which I would've liked to get to know a little better. Instead, I settled for nodding at the blatant *come-hither* looks I received from one eager woman after another.

Something told me getting chewed out by my father wouldn't be nearly as pleasant as what I could get up to with one of these willing partners.

The night was warm but still cooler without so much body heat pressing in from all sides. After signaling the valet, I rechecked my phone. The text wasn't any more pleasant than it had been when I first read it, and my jaw ached thanks to my grinding teeth.

The arrogant asshole.

He snapped his fingers and expected me to come running.

If I was, it was only to spare Mom his ranting over me. She didn't deserve that. If he had something to say, he could tell it to my fucking face.

Earlier tonight, I broke up with a coke addict who would only end up causing further embarrassment, yet somehow, my father would find a way to make me the villain.

Once the car arrived and I tipped the valet, I slid behind the wheel and wrapped my hands around the leather. It was a satisfying feeling, something like regaining control after the shame I would be blamed for heaping on my family only hours ago. The Bugatti shot forward like a bullet from a gun, tearing through the night. I liked to drive fast. I didn't have time to waste, even when I had no doubt I'd get my ass handed to me once I arrived at my destination.

It had been years since I'd moved out of the penthouse my parents shared. Yet, pulling the car into the familiar parking garage felt like stepping back into the past. I moved on autopilot, parking in one of the family's designated spots. My parents' cars were present, along with the pair of black BMWs they used when they required a driver, the other reserved for my sister, Sienna. At least Dad hadn't called her in to witness my assassination.

I rolled my eyes and sighed as I exited the car and headed for the elevator. At least I'd had the presence of mind to stop home and change before meeting the guys, or else I would've reeked like the dirty martini Veronica had thrown at me before the fight had really heated up.

I was twenty-eight years old and well beyond the point of getting called into Dad's office for a talking-to. Yet there I was, staring at the light over the elevator doors and watching it change as I climbed. Once the final floor was illuminated, a soft ping preceded the doors sliding open.

It didn't come as a surprise to find Mom pacing the wide hall leading from the elevator to the living room. She was dressed in workout clothes, and I remembered she took some fitness class with my Aunt Evelyn a few nights a week. Something told me it wasn't yoga or Pilates that had her looking flushed.

"There you are," Mom hissed, coming to a halt with her fists on her hips. "What were you thinking? I told you I didn't like that girl." She barely stopped short of shaking a finger at me as I approached.

"I had a feeling it was something to do with that," I murmured before groaning. "I can explain. You know I wouldn't do anything like that without a reason."

Mom held up both hands, shaking her head. "I don't want to hear it, and I don't need to. It's your father who wants to talk to you about this. He's waiting in his study," she said as if I needed to be told.

"What's the temper on a scale of one to ten?" I asked, arching an eyebrow as I turned my head to gaze down the hall leading from the living room deeper into the penthouse.

"Roughly fifteen," she whispered as her lips drew into a thin line. "And that's after I talked him down from level thirty. He's very, *very* upset. Don't say something you can't take back," she added in a frantic whisper as I began crossing the room.

"I hope you told *him* that," I muttered, squaring my shoulders as I walked. Now, I knew how a condemned man felt during that final walk down the tiled hall, heading toward certain doom.

Instead of striding through the partly open door all at once, I paused. Years of going toe-to-toe with the man had taught me a few things about how to best deal with him. The less I said, the better. I loosened my jaw and pulled in a deep breath, preparing myself to go blank-faced, if only to piss him off.

"Are you going to take all night out there?" Dad's voice was loud and sharp. "Believe me, this won't get any easier for you if you keep me waiting."

The prick. I continued on and pushed the door open before striding into the familiar room. Instead of leaving it a single room devoted to work, Dad removed the wall between it and the room next door, turning it into more of a man cave. It had evolved over the years, but the old arcade games and pool tables were still in place. However, the home theater system had been greatly improved as technology advanced.

It was no surprise he wasn't in the mood to shoot a game of pool or screw around with his new VR headset. He sat behind his desk, a glass of scotch in hand, still dressed for work in one of his typical suits, though he had removed his tie and popped the top two buttons on his crisp shirt. After running a hand through his gray-flecked dark hair, he motioned for me to come closer. "I would ask if you would like a drink..." he began in a tight voice, "... but I understand you've already been on a tour of Manhattan's most popular night spots this evening."

I offered as much of a shrug as I felt like managing. "She came back from the bathroom with white powder around her nostrils. I reminded her that was a dealbreaker for me. She threw a drink in my face. It went downhill from there." With another shrug, I added, "Who knew there was a substance out there more addictive than I am?"

His inscrutable expression left me wondering whether he'd believe me. Probably not. It went against his nature. "Your Uncle Connor did me the favor of calling me to give me the heads-up. It will be front-and-center tomorrow morning across all social media platforms and online outlets," he growled out before spinning the computer so I could read the headline:

Son Of Manhattan Construction Billionaire In A Public Brawl With A Supermodel

Not the family's proudest moment." He took a sip from his glass, eyeing me as he did. I was twenty-eight, too old for the sight of his disappointment to sting, but I had to fight off a flinch just the same. I couldn't remember a time he hadn't demanded more from me than I was able to give.

"The family will get over it." When I stepped toward one of the leather chairs in front of his desk, he cleared his throat loudly.

"I don't remember asking you to sit," he reminded me in a tight voice that felt a lot like a slap across the face. "And this little fiasco tonight wasn't the reason I wanted to see you. Though it's probably the perfect segue," he observed, staring into his tumbler and swirling what was left inside.

"What does that mean?" I dropped into the chair anyway and tried to ignore the way his voice had quieted to something closer to a slither. It raised countless red flags.

"I've let you get away with this for too long," he quietly mused, still observing his liquor in favor of looking at his son. "I told myself you would grow up and stop recklessly bedding and discarding women."

Staring at him while he sat in judgment of me for doing nothing more than what he'd done in his day was the straw that broke the camel's back. "I'm not giving up women for the sake of the family," I flatly informed him. "It's not going to happen."

"That's not an excuse for bumming around with no direction. No goals." Lowering his brow, he growled out,

"Bedding every woman you brush up against doesn't count as a goal."

There wasn't much I hated more than hypocrisy. I knew damn well what a notorious reputation he had when he was my age. There was a reason Mom and her friends had a special nickname for the great Barrett Black and his crew. The hunk holes. I couldn't let it go. "It was for you at one point," I muttered.

"Watch it." I could barely see his eyes, they were so narrow. "I was still running the business at that point. I built it from the ground up. Yes, I played hard, but I worked twice as hard. You keep this up, and that trust fund of yours might just be revoked."

A shock wave rolled through me at the threat. Of all things, I never expected that. "You would cut me off?" I asked, stunned. I always knew he was a self-important prick, but this was a new low, even for him.

He shook his head firmly. "I would never cut you off. I would, however, restrict your access to the assets. There's a reason the trust is revocable versus irrevocable."

He had me by the balls. The worst part was he knew it. That smug little grin he wore as I processed this and searched my brain for any way out told me so.

I could either fall in line and do as I was told or be cut off. If not exactly cut off, as good as. When I tried to imagine living in some shitty studio apartment in Brooklyn, bile began to rise in my throat. I would have to start budgeting and buying groceries rather than going out for all my meals. I would have to live like a so-called normal person, and the idea repulsed me almost as much as the idea of working.

He sighed before placing the glass on the desk. "It's time to push you out of the nest and force you to fly. I only want the best for you, son."

I didn't like the sound of that. The back of my neck prickled, but I gritted my teeth to fight off any obvious reaction. "Meaning?"

A slow, taunting smile spread across his face. "You're going to work in the family business, and I've already set up your first project."

Fuck me.

2

ROSE

"He's going to be late." I rechecked my watch and frowned. We were supposed to meet at eleven thirty, and it was already 11:25. What a surprise. The spoiled little rich boy couldn't be bothered to show up on time.

"Pumpkin, relax. You have nothing to worry about." It was easy for my father to say that, sitting at his desk, completely secure in his position, not only with the company but in the world. He was settled and established. Me? I was stuck with no choice but to hand the most important project of my life so far to a man whose presence I couldn't stand. He was the symbol of everything I hated most about the spoiled little boys I had grown up around. The fact that I gave him my first kiss made me want to go back and strangle that version of myself. Then again, how could I have known?

It took experience to understand that there were selfish, irresponsible, lazy men who could also be charming and fun to hang around. I couldn't understand, back then, how toxic those men could be.

"I want this to go perfectly," I admitted to Dad as I slowly crossed his office. The biggest of them all, of course, was situated in the front corner of the floor. Manhattan stretched out stunningly on two sides of the room with floor-to-ceiling windows that used to almost scare me when I was little. I didn't like heights or being so close to the clouds.

Instead of admiring the view, I gazed up at the portrait of my great-grandmother Dad had hung in his office. They'd had a very special, close relationship. She was more of a mother to him than his mother ever was. It was only since Farrah's passing that the two of them had gotten a little closer, but at least five years had passed since I had seen my grandmother.

"What are you thinking?" Dad's voice was low, full of the fatherly affection he had shown me all my life.

I glanced his way over my shoulder before turning back to the portrait. The woman staring down at me was self-possessed. Almost regal. Impeccable. I recognized the curve of my own mouth in hers, and the steely blue eyes reflected back at me every day in the mirror. "I'm not really thinking," I admitted. "Sometimes, I like to look at her. She reminds me how far I could go if I really wanted to."

"Hell, I could tell you that much," Dad said with a laugh. "Just ask me. I'll tell you you could rule the world one day. You can do anything."

"Isn't that something all parents say to their kids?" I asked with a skeptical smirk, turning toward him.

"Maybe," he allowed with a dip of his chin. "But I mean it. I've known since you were a little girl that you could lead an army into battle if it came to that. Whatever you set your mind to, it's yours."

"Sure, but nobody lives in a vacuum, do they?" Folding

my arms, I pointed out, "We have to rely on other people to, you know, make it to a meeting on time."

His phone rang, and he picked up the receiver while holding up a finger. "Yes? Wonderful."

He checked his watch, smirking. "Send him right in," he said before hanging up and buttoning his navy suit jacket.

11:29. Colton Black liked to cut things close. My blood pressure was beginning to rise, and every thud of my heart against my ribs made my head throb. He was going to be the death of me, and we hadn't started work yet.

Relax. You can handle him. It didn't matter who he was. His past didn't matter, neither did ours. Not that we had a past.

Only one kiss.

The brief memory turned my blood to ice and made my stomach churn. I looked down at my suit and brushed off lint that probably wasn't there.

It had taken a solid hour to decide what to wear today before I'd spent another hour on my hair and makeup. I needed to be impeccable. I needed to set expectations from the jump.

I was in charge.

I knew what I was doing.

All he had to do was follow orders and keep the workers in line.

It was amazing. The things I could tell myself when I needed a little confidence. All that flew straight out the window the moment Dad's office door opened, and his assistant ushered Colton Black into the room.

When was the last time we had been in the same place?

A year, maybe more. Time wasn't enough to make me forget how gorgeous he was. Nothing short of complete amnesia would do that. His dark, almost swarthy good looks combined with an exceptional body and the graceful way he carried himself were enough to take my breath away in those first moments while he shook Dad's hand and they exchanged a few pleasant words. "Ari, so nice to see you."

There was something I had forgotten, though. Something that slammed into me in the most unpleasant way possible. How could I forget the way his deep voice affected me? Once I caught my breath, my pulse took off at breakneck speed. My palms went clammy. My nipples went hard. Saliva flooded my mouth, and I swallowed quickly before putting on something as close to a smile as I could manage. "Colton." I thrust a hand forward before remembering the clamminess.

It was too late for me to pull back.

Colton's much larger hand wrapped around mine, his forehead wrinkling, but that might have been a trick of the light. It was smooth again when he drawled, "Miss Rose Goldsmith. It's been too long." His rich voice was like velvet or maybe warm honey poured over me.

The telltale heat in my core only got hotter when he flashed a dazzling smile.

Get it together.

I withdrew my hand and resisted the childish impulse to wipe my palm on my skirt. Then, Dad asked us to sit in front of his desk. I settled in but was anything but comfortable, thanks to Colton's nearness.

It had been years since I was young and stupid enough to fall for him. Somehow, his being here after all that time passed hadn't changed a thing.

"There isn't much for us to discuss," Dad announced as he sat in his high-backed chair. He looked like the king of New York that way, sitting on top of everything while the city sprawled behind him. "I was hoping to go over the generalities before Rose walked you through the specifics. She can get you up to speed regarding our needs and timeline."

Dad looked my way, and I had to turn my attention from the cologne Colton was wearing. Whatever it was, it was almost enough to curl my toes. "Yes, I've arranged for lunch in my office," I explained with a brief but courteous smile.

"Wonderful. It would be nice to catch up a little too." Colton crossed one ankle over the other knee—the picture of comfort and confidence. How did he manage it? "Though I should tell you, Dad was generous enough to provide me with the files you already shared. I burned the midnight oil, acquainting myself with your needs."

My cheeks flushed when he looked my way. There couldn't be a double meaning behind his words. Could there? He wouldn't be that stupid. Then again, maybe I was giving him too much credit. I couldn't afford to make that mistake now more than ever.

"That's good to hear!" Dad was all smiles as he turned my way. "I knew this was the right choice. And we do like keeping things like this in the family, don't we? So to speak."

"You know the Goldsmiths are as close to the Black family as my Uncle Connor or Aunt Evelyn," Colton reminded him with all kinds of warmth and charm. Meanwhile, I sat there wondering whether ten years had changed the taste of his lips.

I shook it off in a hurry when he shone his warmth on me. "And Rose, here, is practically my sister."

"She's practically your sister." He was screwing with me, using the words his mother had when she found us that night after his birthday party.

Until she'd come outside, it had been the most exciting, incredible moment of my life. The fulfillment of every naïve schoolgirl fantasy. Colton had been starring in them for years, ever since I was old enough to start noticing boys. Until then, he had been the only one I ever so much as looked at.

But then Lourde had found us. In the end, it didn't matter because before dawn the following morning, he'd already moved on to another girl. Some nameless nobody he'd been photographed groping in an after-hours club he'd been too young to visit.

I had cried for a week.

When I forced myself to meet his gaze, humor twinkled in his dark eyes. I wasn't going to flinch. I would not back down. "That must be why I keep getting the urge to give you noogies," I retorted with a sweet smile.

The slight widening of his eyes was more satisfying than any kiss could be. What, he thought I was going to sit back and let him taunt me on my home turf? Obviously, I had made a mistake and overplayed my hand at some point. He knew how I felt about him, or at least how my feelings had changed. He might have been a complete idiot, but he wasn't stupid. He'd noticed how I went out of my way to avoid him.

If he were waiting for me to crumble like a stale piece of cake in the face of his magnetism, he would be waiting a long time.

"Colton, we are so glad to be working with you." If my father had any hesitations about this, he did his best to hide them. Standing, he reached out to shake Colton's hand again. "I have nothing but faith in you, you know." Damn, if he didn't sound like he meant it too. I couldn't fathom how.

"Thank you, sir," Colton replied. "If only my father saw it like you do."

The men shared a knowing grin. They both understood

Barrett well. "He wouldn't assign you this project if he didn't know you could handle it. Besides..." Dad added, winking at me, "... Rose here will keep everything in line."

"I have no doubt." Colton looked my way and raised his brows in expectation. "Well? I'm in your hands," he offered.

If that were true, I would have to start using more sanitizer. Who knew where he had been? "I'll show you to my office," I offered as I stood. I hope sandwiches and salad will be all right for lunch."

Colton laughed. "Are you kidding? It will be the most nourishing meal I've had lately. It turns out the olives from a martini don't count as a serving of vegetables." Dad had to go and laugh at Colton's weak joke, which, of course, only encouraged him. I settled on leading the way out the door without bothering to wait for him to join me.

He would have to follow me.

He'd better hope he can keep up.

It was only when he fell in step behind me that I realized he was probably looking at my ass. I came within a heartbeat of swinging my hips before stopping myself. Things would be bad enough without me egging him on. The last thing I wanted was for him to think I was deliberately teasing.

"That's a nice suit," he murmured almost too softly. It was barely audible, but the meaning was obvious. That was all I was to him—someone to have fun with, like the empty-headed girls he usually preyed on. The ones who didn't bother looking beneath that gorgeous, perfectly put-together façade. If they ever had, they would have found nothing. Emptiness.

"So, how come I never see you around town?" he asked in a breezy, carefree tone as we entered my office. "I run into your twin cousins, Aria and Valentina, all the time."

Sliding his hands into the pockets of his slacks, he gave the room an approving look. "I even run into my sister sometimes," he continued, taking in the blown-up fashion sketches on the walls—vintage designs from the company's early days. "But never you. Don't tell me you've been avoiding me all this time."

Colton didn't get it. He still thought this was a big joke—an excuse to flirt, to exploit our longtime acquaintance. There wasn't a doubt in my mind that he figured he'd get off easy, thanks to that connection. He probably imagined he would coast by and take credit for the project's success. It was enough to make me boil.

"Let's get one thing straight." Folding my arms, I lifted my chin, staring at him head-on. I wouldn't give him an excuse to joke about me avoiding him ever again. That was a mistake, and I couldn't afford to make any with Colton Black. "We're not here to screw around, and I'm not charmed as easily as my dad. If you make another comment about my suit or anything else about me, I'll have you kicked off this project. Got it?" He was lucky I bit my tongue before threatening to kick him in the balls while I was at it. I was damn proud of my self-control, along with my strength. The wide-eyed teenager was long gone, and it was about time he figured it out.

I didn't expect him to cower.

I didn't expect him to roll over and show me his belly like a submissive puppy.

I also didn't expect the slow, knowing grin my warning inspired.

Somehow, I had flipped a switch, and all at once, the professional image dropped away to reveal the Colton I'd known was waiting all along. "Careful, now," he growled out, his flashing eyes moving up and down my body. "Maybe

I like it when a woman gets mouthy. You'd better stop getting me excited, or we won't be able to get any work done at all."

I should have ordered him out, called my father's office, and refused to go through with the arrangement. What did I do instead? I blushed to the roots of my hair and had to consciously keep my knees from shaking under the weight of his seductive stare. Much more of this, and I'd be begging him to take me on my desk—repeatedly.

He wouldn't make it easy to keep things professional.

If this were any indication, it would be downright impossible.

But come hell or high water, I *would* resist him.

3

COLTON

If this kept up much longer, I'd have to put that smart mouth of hers to better use.

Her haughty, bossy attitude was getting to me. Nobody talked to me like that. The bitchier she got, the more determined I became to break her down. It would take nothing to get her purring like a kitten.

My comments were enough to make her drop the bitch act long enough for me to see the truth. The girl standing in front of me was defenseless, though she was also stubborn enough to pretend otherwise. She tossed her head back, and I caught her blonde hair's light, sweet scent.

Hunger rolled through me like a wave, leaving me with the urge to bury my face in her neck and commit her to memory, but I couldn't go around drooling over her. "Do you think that's funny?" she asked coldly.

"Does it sound like I'm joking?" I countered. "Let's get one thing straight, you and me. I didn't come here to get scolded like a bad little boy, and I know this isn't fun and games. But I won't walk around on my tiptoes, afraid to be real. We aren't strangers, Rose."

She had perfected the disparaging eye roll. Only my sister, Sienna, was better at it than Rose. "Don't think you're going to use that against me," she warned, and the disgust behind it made my blood simmer.

The fuck was her problem?

I could barely swallow my irritation to choke out, "How would I use it against you? Isn't this the way the world works? People who know each other work together, or they recommend each other to their network. Where is the crime in working alongside someone you grew up with?"

The way she frowned stirred my interest, like she was expecting something else. What did she want me to say? I figured I had her pegged, and for the most part, I was right.

Rose was the ice queen whose shit didn't stink, holding herself superior to me.

Beyond that, though, there was something else going on. I would have sworn there was a humming in the air as I took one step toward her, then another. The sound intensified the closer I got until she had no choice but to back away in one big, decisive step. "I'm not going to bite," I murmured, my eyes moving over her once again as I imagined what was hiding under that buttoned-up suit.

She barked out a laugh. "Good thing, since I don't know when I had my last rabies shot."

I touched a hand to my chest like her words stung when all they did was leave me wanting to throw her over the desk and fuck the attitude out of her. "What did I do to deserve this?"

"Maybe it's not what you've done, but who you've done," she retorted, her green eyes going wide like something came out she never intended to voice. After sputtering for a second, she quickly retracted, "That was a low blow. I shouldn't have said it."

"That would be a nice apology if it was one." I took too much pleasure in the way she flinched but fuck her and her superiority bullshit. "But I'm an expert at going out of my way not to apologize, so you can't fool me."

"Let's move past it, okay?" There was a slight tremor in her voice by the time she practically fled to her desk and settled in behind it.

Did it make her feel stronger doing that?

I would've bet on it.

"Please, have a seat," she invited, motioning to the chairs in front of her desk. "Lunch should be here any minute. As Dad said, we need to go over our schedule. We purposely baked a little extra time into it." She tapped on her keyboard as she spoke, squinting a little as she studied the screen. "You said you've familiarized yourself with what's already been put together?

I heard her. Every word was crystal clear. Yet somehow, when she looked at me from across the desk, I drew a blank. *What was the question?* I would have much rather talked about how her suit clung to every curve and molded itself over her body like liquid. My hands damn near twitched when I imagined running them over those curves, testing their firmness, indulging in her full hips and ass. When I thought back to when we were kids, I remembered a gawky, shy girl whose nose was always in a book. "How did you end up here?" I asked instead.

The widening of her eyes told me the question surprised her as much as it did me. I hadn't meant to ask, but since she didn't shut me down immediately, I took it as a sign she was willing to drop the imperious bitch act for a little bit.

"I mean, how does anybody end up anywhere?" she countered, folding her hands on the desk. Long, slim fingers. I could practically feel them wrapped around my shaft, which incidentally began to thicken as the fantasy swirled in my head.

"Was it an ultimatum? Do this, or else?" I asked, remembering my most recent conversation with Dad.

It seemed like my questions had their intended effect. The ice began to melt, and the soft laughter tumbling from her ruby lips had a nice, melodic quality. It was something I could get used to if she'd loosen up. "No!" She chuckled. "I wanted to do this. I always have. Or don't you remember?"

How could I have forgotten? That night in Vail, Christmas break, we were sitting by the campfire outside the cabin. The two of us, fifteen and seventeen, were talking about nothing important and everything at the same time. She made it easy to open up.

Sitting with her now, I recalled the confession she'd made.

"I want to be the best. I want to be just like my great-grandmother. I want to be a legend one day like she is."

Even back then, when most of the blood that should have been in my brain was usually making my dick hard whenever the wind blew the right way, I sensed her sincerity. I heard the determination. There wasn't a question in my mind of whether or not she would do exactly what she said.

"Of course," I said. "Vail. That was a good night. It's a shame you decided I wasn't worth talking to anymore as we both grew up, or we could've done more of that." Did I sound bitter? So what if I did?

Her mouth fell open before snapping shut. "Yes. It's a shame." She turned her attention back to the laptop, sitting up so straight I wouldn't have been surprised if there was a broomstick down the back of her jacket. All it would take was slicking her golden blonde hair back and putting on a pair of thick glasses, and she would make the perfect disapproving teacher or stern librarian.

Stand down. My dick was entirely too interested in that scenario. It seemed like he was interested in everything she did.

Before I could figure out what I did wrong this time, a girl I assumed was Rose's assistant discreetly rolled our lunch in on a cart. "Thank you," Rose offered. "You can leave it by the window."

"Can I get you anything else?" The girl looked my way, and what happened next was no surprise. Her eyes traveled over me quickly, efficiently sizing me up before her glossy lips curved in an inviting smile—a familiar one too.

"What's your name?" I asked, extending my hand. "I'm Colton Black."

"Natalie," she greeted, placing her hand in mine and squeezing it.

"Well, Natalie, this lunch looks great." Not as great as she did in a tight-fitting black dress that fit her like a glove and left little to the imagination. Nice tits. Natural, by the looks of them, balanced well with full hips that begged to be gripped from behind. I deepened my voice and widened my smile. "Thank you for bringing it in. I'm sure we'll get to know each other a little better while I'm working on this project with Miss Goldsmith. You'll get sick of the sound of my voice," I predicted, drawing a soft giggle.

She was hot, but the women who worked at Goldsmith Couture always were. It was an image thing. The plainest girl was encouraged to step up her game, dress and groom impeccably, and represent the company well. Natalie fit the bill, even if she was only one of dozens of others in this very building. Rose Goldsmith was a successful model before she decided to throw that career away and be a businesswoman. Not that I secretly followed her modeling career unbeknownst to her brother.

"Is there anything else?" Rose's sharp question made Natalie drop my hand as if it burned.

"No." The girl shook her head hard enough to make her brown ponytail swing. "So long as everything is set up here."

"It is." Rose's smile was hard enough I was surprised she didn't crack a tooth. "That will be all."

I waited until Natalie left us alone before releasing a high-pitched whistle. "Damn."

Rose's head snapped around to level a fiery glare my way. "What?" she challenged in a tight voice.

Shrugging, I replied, "There I was, thinking you were only bitchy toward me. I'm disappointed."

"We don't pay people to hang around and socialize." She got up and went to the cart, keeping her back to me. Did she think that would hide the rapid way her shoulders rose and fell? "Feel free to help yourself."

If she knew I was staring at her ass when she said it, she would've chosen different words. I would've liked very much to help myself to that juicy peach. There was something about a woman in a suit that did things to me a naked woman had never come close to. It just so happened the woman in question excited more than my dick, though he got that excited too, so much so that I had to look away or else risk showing off a hard-on when I got up to get my food.

I should tell her to get it for me. The idea made me snicker before she turned around and hit me with an angry stare. "What's so funny?" she demanded.

Damn, she was wound tight. Nothing a nice, long fuck

wouldn't take care of, but I wasn't about to suggest it and end up with a bottle of sparkling water poured over my head. "Are you always ready to bite somebody's head off?" I asked rather than propositioning her.

Now, I knew one way to get rid of a semi in a hurry. Being glared at like my head would look better on a spike in the middle of Central Park did the trick.

Her cheeks went pink before she turned back to her desk. "No. I mean, forget it," she mumbled as she sat. I couldn't get a read on her any more than I could understand why it mattered either way. She insisted on acting like she had something to prove, though I couldn't imagine what.

I got up and grabbed a sandwich without bothering to check what kind it was. I could eat just about anything. That morning, I had skipped breakfast which wasn't uncommon since I was rarely awake.

But today, I had to get up on time like a good boy, like Daddy's little soldier, and my empty stomach reminded me of the change in my schedule. "I have an idea," I suggested while unwrapping what turned out to be a turkey and Swiss on rye. "Why don't we talk about the project?"

"Wow." She widened her eyes. "That's actually a sensible suggestion."

I had always liked Ari and didn't want to ruin our relationship. But enough was enough.

"Drop the attitude." I turned around, glad to be quick enough to watch her mouth fall open. "I might not be anybody's idea of a great businessman. I don't want to be. But something tells me we're not going to get anywhere if all you do is put me down, criticize me for chatting with one of your employees, and threaten me with getting moved off the project."

By the time she cleared her throat, I was seated again, my plate on her desk and a napkin across my lap. "Maybe you're right," she agreed, her voice devoid of smug superiority. I'm way too uptight over this project. It means a lot to me that it goes off without a hitch. It's my big shot at something real."

For the first time since we laid eyes on each other in Ari's office, she was being honest—no barbs, no snark, no judgment. The ice queen had been replaced by someone real and vulnerable. Though I couldn't relate to wanting to work, I could respect how serious she was.

"We'll get it right," I promised. The words fell out of my mouth before I could stop them. Not that I cared about her project as much as I cared about getting her to ease up.

"Thank you." She bit her lip before picking up her fork and stabbing at the lettuce in her bowl. "Before we go any further with project talk, be honest with me. I was honest with you."

She wanted honesty? I was honestly turned on by the way she licked a bit of dressing off the corner of her mouth, but something told me that wasn't the sort she was looking for. "About what?" I asked, shifting in my chair thanks to the discomfort caused by the tightness in my boxer briefs.

My strength started waning, and we had been alone for fifteen minutes. How was I supposed to survive a month with her?

"Why are you doing this?" she asked. "And does it have something to do with the little fight that hit the tabloids this morning? *International Model Has A Public Brawl With Billionaire's Playboy Son?*" She was enjoying this, trying not to grin before taking a mouthful of greens and grilled chicken.

"It wasn't a brawl," I muttered. "She got pissed off, threw

a drink in my face, and we screamed at each other. I don't think that qualifies as a brawl."

"It does if the media knows certain last names will be clickbait," she pointed out with a hint of sympathy and understanding. In that way, she reminded me of her brother. Noah would bust my balls over something like this, but he would then take my side the way she seemed to be doing.

The last thing I wanted to think about while lusting after Rose was her older brother, so I pushed all thoughts of him aside in favor of watching her eat. She did it with gusto, refusing to waste time by picking slowly at her food. She was someone who didn't waste time pretending much of anything.

It was almost refreshing.

"Is there something on my face?" I only realized I'd been ogling her openly once she started patting her chin and lips. "Something wrong?"

"I zoned out," I replied, and it wasn't a lie. "You look... great. Perfect."

Her lips parted so she could take in a short breath. "Oh. Thank you," she whispered. "You don't have to say that. You already have the job, remember?" A shaky laugh punctuated the statement, but her gaze was unflinching.

Those eyes of hers. I couldn't get enough of their brilliance.

"A comment like that won't get me fired, will it?" I asked to break the tension. It would get me nowhere, pursuing the invisible third party sitting between us—an all-consuming desire. *Damn, I need to get laid.* I had a job to do, not to mention the thought of Noah reminding me of our friendship. He'd kick my ass in a heartbeat if he knew a fraction of what was going through my head when I looked at her.

She rolled her eyes, throwing a withering look my way.

"Don't press your luck. That's all I'm going to say." She didn't have me fooled. I could see through her. She was trying her hardest to resist me. Any number of women could have told her that was pointless, but it's not like I wanted to waste time getting in touch with any of them. Not when I had her in front of me, standing gracefully to return to the cart for a bottle of water.

Something shot me out of my seat. I had no idea whether I was more interested in being close to her or observing the effect my nearness would have. No way did she mean it when she was cold, distant, and dismissive. I refused to believe it. She was a red-blooded woman like any other, and no one could ever resist me when I had them in my crosshairs.

"Excuse my reach," I murmured, leaning over the cart to grab a bottle of Perrier.

People did it all the time, placing a hand against the back of the person beside them as they crowded in. I kept it light and casual until our hands brushed. The spark that leaped from her hand to mine was a far cry from the clammy handshake I'd received earlier.

Rose stiffened with a gasp. "Sorry," she whispered, pulling her hand back. "Take what you want."

Well? She'd asked for it. I was only doing as I was told.

Her sharp intake of breath paired well with my needful groan when I used the hand on her back to pull her closer. "I thought you'd never ask," I murmured with a grin.

She tipped her head back to search my face, her green eyes swirling with surprise and confusion. "What are you doing?" she asked, her tone breathy as she went stiff against me.

"What you said. I'm taking what I want." With my free hand, I hooked a finger under her chin, studying her face.

One hundred Renaissance masters could not have captured her almost perfectly symmetrical features, her peaches and cream complexion, and the faint sprinkling of freckles she tried and failed to cover up. They told the story of her life, how she tried to hide her true self in favor of who she thought she had to be.

This had started as a little bit of fun, a way to throw her off-balance and remind her who was in charge, yet now I struggled not to lose myself in her beauty.

"You shouldn't do this." Her voice was firm but soft. All the indignation she'd thrown at me when we first entered her office had drained away. It encouraged me, and so did her choice of words.

She didn't say no, did she?

"Shouldn't do what? This?" Tracing the curve of her jaw with my fingertips left her closing her eyes and swaying closer. "Or this?" My thumb brushed over her pouty lips. What I wouldn't give to feel them wrapped around my cock while her golden head bobbed.

"It's not right." Her eyes opened slowly, but there was even less resolve in them now. Her voice sounded pretty damn weak too. I knew it. She hadn't changed, no matter how she pretended otherwise.

"Since when has that ever stopped me?" I asked with a soft chuckle, lowering my head, prepared to taste her tempting lips.

Before I could, her eyes went hard. I'd made a mistake. Before I could correct myself, she placed a hand against my chest and pushed. "Colton." She was barely breathing, gasping for air like she had come back from a run or finished coming on my tongue. "If we're going to work together, we need to get something straight. This is a professional relationship. I don't mix business and pleasure, *ever*."

"Neither do I," I reminded her, snickering. "But that's usually because I don't give a fuck about business."

She didn't find it funny. No, in fact, her frown deepened. "I'm serious. This isn't going to happen. Besides, I'm... involved with someone."

Idiot. Fucking idiot. Just like that, the moment was over, and I released her before taking a backward step. "You might've saved me a lot of time and told me that in the first place."

Dammit.

What was I doing?

Rolling her eyes, she retorted, "I didn't think I'd have to since I don't normally announce my relationship status to people I work with." She made a big deal of straightening her suit jacket, though I hadn't done a damn thing to it. She even ran her hands over her blonde bob to smooth it down.

I didn't know what pissed me off worse, my assumption or the fact that she made a point. She had no reason to announce she had a boyfriend until I forced her hand.

If I were going to prove Dad wrong, I couldn't afford to fall into my old traps. Rose Goldsmith may as well have been wearing a sign with the word *Trap* written in neon across her tits.

"My apologies." That wasn't the first time I'd been rejected, even if this particular rejection stung in a way none of the others had. But I was an adult, and so was she. It was better not to shit where I ate, anyway.

Returning to my chair, I picked up what was left of my sandwich. "So let's talk scheduling. I understand we want to start on Monday. What do you think about me going out there sometime this weekend to get a look at the existing structure?"

She trained her wary gaze on me as she found her seat

and lowered herself slowly. "What about Sunday? We could meet there."

"Works for me." I glanced her way and found her arching an eyebrow. "Don't worry. From now on, we're all business."

Now, if only somebody could give my dick the memo.

4

ROSE

"Honey? Are you okay?" Only then did I realize Mom was staring at me with a concerned expression. "Are you feeling all right?" she asked while her brows drew together.

I knew that look well. It was one of her favorites.

"I'm fine," I lied, raising my voice to be heard over the Friday night dinner crowd. "Distracted, is all."

"I'm glad you had the time for dinner with your old mom." She lifted her glass of merlot my way, showing off her toned arms. "And I respect the hell out of you for working so hard. Your dad is ready to burst. He's so excited to watch you put this new store together."

If anything, I was relieved she assumed it was the store I was thinking about. That was a much safer explanation than the truth. I had spent the past six hours in a fog, unable to steer my thoughts away from Colton—his dark eyes, voice, and hair that practically begged me to run my fingers through it.

And strong.

He was very strong. All it had taken was a hand against

my back, and I was almost pinned against his unforgiving chest.

All right, so I didn't exactly fight very hard to avoid being pinned. That only made things worse. I was too overwhelmed to react right away and too damn wet.

"Hello?" Mom waved a hand in front of my face. "I'm starting to take it personally. What do I have to do to hold your attention?"

"I'm sorry, really," I insisted. This was not the time or the place to indulge in fantasizing. There would be plenty of time for that later, at home. Maybe with the help of my vibrator, though I doubted it would be necessary. Not when I had already spent the better part of the day painfully aroused and ready to beg someone to touch me to relieve the tension.

"Don't get me wrong." She looked and sounded like a woman who knew what she was talking about because she did. "The thrill of success is a drug. It's right up there with love, just as addictive and dangerous if you let yourself fall out of balance with it. You can't forget the rest of the world just because you're in love, and you can't forget it just because you're good at your job. You'll always end up missing out on something else that could be just as fulfilling."

I nudged the rest of my grilled salmon to the side, folding my arms on the edge of the table and leaning in. "How did you do it? You always had everything in balance. Both of you did. I mean, you never missed an activity or a concert. Do you know how many kids never had parents in the audience?" I could still remember those kids, watching them scan the audience, their foreheads furrowed. I never had to worry about that, yet my parents both ran wildly successful companies.

I knew her too well to think she would accept a compliment without trying to brush it away first, so it didn't surprise me when she laughed lightly and shook her head. "I'm glad you remember it that way. Don't get me wrong, Dad and I did our best. But it took roughly the same amount of planning as the invasion of Normandy, and I still lost nights of sleep, telling myself I was screwing everything up and failing you two." She blew out a soft sigh before taking a sip of her wine.

I would never have known. "Way to go," I told her. "You gave me another reason why you were the best mom ever. You made it look easy."

"Anyway," she continued, waving me off. "I don't want to see you miss out on anything. You know I admire your intensity and single-mindedness, but there is such a thing as overdoing it. You're too young to devote all your time to work. I know you have goals, but you also have time. Plenty of it."

This wasn't the first time she had given me a speech like that. It always ended with her calling me intense and praising me for it but warning me against it at the same time.

Tonight, I had a way to counter that. "For your information, I'm in the middle of trying to catch somebody's eye. So I'm not only thinking about work." Did I feel a little smug? Maybe.

It was Mom's turn to push her plate aside and lean in. She was a remarkable person, but she was a typical mother in many ways. Her eyes danced as she asked, "Who? Do I know them? What do they do for a living?"

My thoughts drifted to an article in the *Times* of the man of the hour. A man announced his candidacy for the state senate today.

Landon Jones, twenty-eight, graduated Summa Cum Laude from Harvard University before moving on to Harvard Law School, where he served as editor of the Harvard Law Review before graduating at the top of his class...

He was Mr. Perfect. The man had it all—golden good looks, dazzlingly blue eyes, and a jaw that looked like it had been carved from granite. He had the sure, confident smile of a born winner. All of that, combined with his ambition, his father's prominence as a circuit court judge, and his mother's background in high society and philanthropic endeavors, practically assured him a win on voting day.

"I'm only trying to get his attention. It's not time to start the wedding registry yet." I sort of liked letting her dangle for a little bit. Besides, I didn't want to oversell it. The idea was to get her to stop worrying and criticizing. That was all. "It's not a big deal. But... you know the name."

She blew out a frustrated sigh. "Honey, I know a lot of names. You're going to need to be more specific."

I searched my memory while sipping Chablis before offering, "You've served on a few committees with his mom."

"Again. That narrows it down to roughly a hundred people."

Finally, it hit me. She'd have to get it now. "He was in the news recently."

She almost slammed herself back into her chair, and I told myself I must be hallucinating the look of horror twisting her features and draining the color from her face. My heart dropped like a rock before a half-dozen ugly, gruesome scenarios raced through my mind. Was he secretly a murderer or something? Did he have a dark past Mom knew about?

I started to feel a little defensive before long. "Okay, I think I could do a lot worse," I grumbled when she continued staring at me like I had mutilated myself somehow. "I thought you would like the idea of me being a state senator's girlfriend."

Her lashes fluttered before she shook herself. "Hang on. State senator? Who are you talking about?"

"Landon Jones." I huffed. "You've served on committees with Mrs. Jones. And you and Dad have been to parties at the Jones' estate plenty of times."

Her eyes bulged before she clapped a hand over her mouth. When she lowered it, laughter burst out of her loudly enough that we grabbed the attention of a few diners at a nearby table. She was too busy dabbing away tears from the corners of her eyes to notice.

"I'm sorry," she eventually choked out before sipping some water. Once she'd gotten a hold of herself, she explained. "Why in the world did my mind immediately go to Colton?"

In the blink of an eye, I was a kid again. Guilty, afraid my mother could see straight through me. There were certain things she did not need to know about, and this newfound lust for Colton Black was at the top of the list.

Her reaction alone was reason enough to make me sure of that.

"Colton?" I wrinkled my nose and shuddered. "I'm insulted." Did I sound convincing? I needed to.

"But you have to admit, it fits. I'm certainly familiar with the name. I've served on committees with Lourde plenty of times. I know the family, and Colton was in the news today," she concluded before polishing off the rest of her wine.

"You've put together a compelling case, attorney," I joked. "But you should still know better. I can't think of two people more opposite than Landon and Colton. I'm tired of dating idiots, Mom."

She frowned, only wanting the best for me. "Like your ex, Morgan? I never liked him."

I let out a weary sigh. "Morgan was gorgeous, intelligent, and a lot of fun. I'd told myself we had a future. It seemed like my drive and work ethic rubbed off on him, at least for a while. It wasn't long before I figured out he was more interested in being attached to the Black name than me. I'm so sick of playboys with no ambition except to spend their trust fund or mine!"

"I hear you when it comes to Morgan, honey, but perhaps Landon and Colton aren't so entirely different," she countered, wearing a fond grin. "He's got a good heart hidden under all that bravado. I bet you didn't know when the hurricane hit last year, Colton was there for a month distributing aid and volunteering to rebuild some homes using his own trust. He cares. Like his father. Like all the hunk holes."

The hunk holes. If I never heard the term again, it would be too soon. The way they turned Dad and his friends, Barrett, Connor, and Magnus into some big myth like there was something charming about sleeping their way through New York in their younger days.

"How many times do I have to remind you I don't love thinking of Dad that way?" I pretended to gag, which only got her laughing again.

"You understand what I mean, though. Appearances can be deceiving."

I could see straight through her motherly advice. Still, I was floored to hear about Colton's philanthropy. "You have a soft spot for him because he and Noah have always been so close." The two of them practically grew up in the other's home, bouncing back and forth together during school breaks for as long as I could remember.

That was why it had been easy to fall for him when I was a kid. He was always around, as much a part of our family as my brother.

Mom lifted a shoulder before dipping into her clutch for her cell. "That could be. I look at him and see the little boy he used to be. All of you. I see all of you as kids. You'll understand one day."

Before I could remind her that day would be years in the future, she gasped at whatever she was reading on her phone. "Dammit! I forgot I was supposed to meet Pepper tonight for a drink. She's waiting for me. I can't cancel now."

It was sort of a relief since the Colton talk needed to end. "Don't worry about it. Go on ahead. We're finished here, anyway," I told her, signaling for the check while pulling out one of my cards. "Besides, I'm supposed to go over to Sienna's. She's having a party."

The relief on Mom's face as she kissed my cheek made up for the little lie. Sienna Black *was* having a party at her apartment in Soho, and I had been invited. I had also spent lunch with her brother earlier, had lied to him about having a boyfriend in a last-ditch effort to keep from making an unforgivably stupid mistake, and had then indulged in some of the filthiest, horniest fantasies imaginable. How was I supposed to look her in the face now?

Not only that, but what if Colton stopped by? They didn't exactly go out of their way to be part of each other's social lives, but they didn't avoid each other, either. They shared a lot of friends. It wasn't beyond the realm of possibility that he would saunter in with some skank hanging on him like a cheap jacket. After the unreal tension between us earlier, I didn't think I could handle that.

I waited until Mom left in the back of a black Lexus before ordering an Uber to take me home. Going over the designs for the store's interior wasn't exactly my idea of a fun on a Friday night, but it was safer than risking another run-in with my first love. It was corny, but I couldn't avoid it. I was in love with him back then, the way only a teenage girl could be. I was idealistic and blind to the red flags, sure that I understood him better than anybody. That I saw his heart, the one Mom had referred to, so certain we shared something special, something for the two of us alone. That was what made me better for him than any girl ever could be.

Poor, deluded kid.

Since those days, I had come too far to risk getting wrapped up in him again. He wasn't worth it back then, and he was not now as I left the restaurant to meet my driver at the curb.

Once I was nestled in the back seat, I texted Sienna.

Me: *Sorry, babe, but I feel a headache coming on. I won't be able to make it tonight. Call me tomorrow and tell me how it went.*

My phone immediately lit up.

Damn.

"Hey, Sie—"

"Uh, no, no way you're bailing on me tonight."

"I'd love to come, but, honestly, this store is really sucking all my energy. I have to be on."

She let out an exaggerated sigh. Being a successful businesswoman herself, I knew she'd get it.

"Really?" she wailed. "Can't my brother pick up the slack?"

I hadn't really discussed my dislike for Colton with Sienna, and I always avoided discussing him.

"He is, but there is a lot on my plate right now. Can we meet up after the store opening?" I pleaded. "You know I want to make my parents proud of this, right?"

"I know, I know. Jesus, all right. No fresh dick for you then." I let out a bark of laughter. "Although, with Landon as your husband-to-be, I wonder if any fresh dick would cut it anyway? Hmm..." she added. "Have you been stalking him again online?"

"Oh, way to go," I grumbled. "Make me sound like a predator."

"Honey, we're talking about the Manhattan scene here. Either you're a predator, or you're prey. Believe me..." she continued, "... not that I would ever blame you for stalking that man. Landon Jones is sex on two legs." I couldn't help but laugh at her assessment, though she wasn't wrong. "But I need to tell you, girl. Now that he's announced his candidacy, the competition is going to get very stiff, very fast. There's a whole city full of women sharpening their claws, ready to sink them in deep."

She wasn't telling me anything I hadn't already considered, but I brushed it off with a laugh. "Whatever. I have a leg up on all of them. Our families have a long friendship, so we're not strangers. And you know there's going to be plenty of fundraisers at his family estate in East Hampton, where I will just so happen to be spending a lot of time once the new store is open."

"You've given this a lot of thought," she noted. "You've really got your sights set on him, huh?"

That was putting it mildly.

"I want something real," I concluded. "I have everything else figured out. My dream job, my dream apartment, and the best friends in the world."

"Thank you very much," she joked. "But I thought you were too busy thinking about the new store to worry about fresh dick."

"It's not like I'm going to be the one laying brick or

installing windows," I retorted. "I think I can handle figuring out a way to get Landon's attention while also overseeing construction."

"Actually, it might help if you ran around in a hardhat, wearing a toolbelt. Landon, can I get your help? I have a screw that needs driving," she announced in a breathy whisper.

I pressed my lips tight together and fought back a grin. "That doesn't even make sense," I pointed out.

"Maybe you could tell him you're looking for fresh wood?"

"Better," I admitted. "But still not quite right."

"Hmm..." She paused. "Something about getting nailed?"

That was what broke me. "Okay," I managed between bursts of laughter.

"I'm going to message you later, and you're going to wish you came to my party!"

And with that, the line went dead, and my thoughts shifted to the wrong man.

If your brother shows up with a girl, don't tell me about that. Because even though I knew Colton Black was all wrong for me and always would be, that didn't mean I needed to hear how easy it was for him to forget me and move on to somebody else.

Again.

It had hurt bad enough when he did it the first time.

5

COLTON

Fuck.

People went out of their way to get up this early?

Dear old Dad.

There he was, sitting in his study, expecting me, and on a Sunday at holy fuck o'clock. Mom was obviously still asleep.

It was a damn good thing I set my alarm earlier than necessary because when I woke, there was a glaring text from Dad demanding my presence before I left for the Hamptons. Not only had he demanded my presence, but he also knew my schedule.

He was keeping tabs on me like I was still a fucking kid, and it pissed me off to no end.

Dad's smug smile widened as he saw me approaching. "Son. Nice to see you at this hour."

"Wish I could say the same," I muttered, dragging my feet into his office and refusing to sit down.

He slid a thick file across his desk, and I narrowed my eyes at him. "Everything is in here to hit the ground running with the store. The four-week schedule, plans and suppliers, plus other ancillary details."

I took it, staring down at him, confused. "You gave those details the other day?"

"Did I now?"

We stared at one another long enough for me to realize the arrogant son-of-a-bitch was testing me.

"If you would have done your homework inside of hand-holding your cock, you would have realized I only gave you the preliminary plans, not the contractor schematics and project plan. You haven't even checked the documents I gave you previously, have you?"

Rage bubbled inside my chest. This was a test. He was testing me all along. He didn't trust me, yet he was forcing me into this shit-storm of a project anyway. "So you decided to set me up to fail anyway?" I pushed out through gritted teeth.

"I don't want you fucking this up for the Goldsmiths. Ari and I are, of course, across this store opening."

"Except the difference is, Ari trusts his daughter implicitly and is proud of her."

All at once, his face hardened, and I knew I was in for it. But fuck it. I wanted no part of any of this, even if working with Rose Goldsmith was a trip down memory lane. It wasn't her brains I was thinking about as I stood in front of my father, doing my best not to react one way or another.

It was her face. Her lithe, firm body.

She wouldn't be able to avoid me this time. It would be the silver lining to this whole fuckup of a situation.

Ever since we had that kiss the night of my eighteenth birthday, she'd existed in the *what-if* section of my memory. But dammit, revisiting the tempting Rose meant following orders, which was something I didn't do. Stubbornness had always been one of my strongest qualities, and the idea of letting my father know I was powerless in all of this left me grinding my teeth while heat flared in my chest.

"Tell me then, what was the point of the time you spent working for the company during your school breaks and after you graduated if you don't do a damn thing with that knowledge? Don't tell me it was all a means of making me happy."

It was a means of getting him off my back, whatever he needed to tell himself. "I'm not a good fit for the business. You told me yourself," I reminded him. That diatribe was burned into my memory, along with another few epic meltdowns following my worst behavior. The sailboat I sank, the expulsions, the disaster that was my twenty-first-birthday weekend. Not that the damage to the cabin was entirely my fault. I couldn't exactly keep track of all my guests at all times. Dad's voice was shot for three days after that one.

He sighed dramatically. "When are you ever going to grow out of the habit of misquoting me? I told you your lack of work ethic and allergy to responsibility wouldn't get you far anywhere you chose to go, my company included. And that's the truth, isn't it? Because I haven't seen you try to make a damn thing of yourself in all of your twenty-eight years."

I could recite all of this without hardly trying. His favorite monologue was all about how he'd fought, scraped, and clawed his way to where he currently sat in a lavish penthouse surrounded by his pricey toys. It was boring as fuck. "I don't know what you want me to say," I said with a shrug once he'd finished reminding me how old I was. "We're not the same."

"No shit."

I walked out, balling my fists at my sides. His snide

laughter followed me down the hall, leaving me clenching my fists and jamming them into my pockets rather than picking up the closest item and throwing it.

My mother was in the kitchen, making a cup of tea. At the sound of my approach, she set down the kettle and turned her full attention my way. How many times had she faced me that way in the moments after a fight with Dad? Anxious, practically folding her hands like she was praying to hear something good. "Morning, sweetheart. I didn't expect you here at this hour," she whispered.

"I didn't have to come this morning, Mom." I kissed her cheek then running a hand through my dark hair, I stared down the hall toward the patch of light streaming from the study. "Where the hell does he get the nerve? Testing me like this?"

Confusion swept her bare face before a gentle smile replaced it. "Whatever your father does, he does it because he loves you and wants what's best for you, Colton."

"Yeah, like cutting me off? He said that the other day, you know…"

"He would never cut you off. Don't exaggerate." That was one thing about Mom. She gave me a lot of leeway, but there were some things she wouldn't let me get away with.

"Fine," I grumbled. "He wants to turn me into a regular person, the way he grew up. It's bullshit."

"It's life." She reached up to pat my cheek and brought me comfort, at least for a moment or two. "And there are worse things in the world than having to work. It's funny. I was just as stubborn as you are but in the opposite way."

She looked happier, so I pursued the topic. "What do you mean?"

"My mother just about threw a fit when I told her I wanted to work." She leaned against the counter, chuckling.

"And believe me, if you think your father is a tough nut to crack, you should have known your grandmother back in the day. It was my dad who told me to go ahead with it." There was fondness in her voice, though I doubt she felt generous at the time.

"Why were you determined to work when you didn't need to?" I asked. She'd grown up the way I had, unlike Dad.

She lifted a shoulder and said, "I wanted something I could be proud of. And I am. I have something for me, something I built along with Auntie Olivia." She insisted on calling her that, even if we weren't related. The fact that we'd spent every waking moment growing up with the Goldsmiths, they may as well count as family. It made sense.

Guess the apple didn't fall far from the tree with Rose as headstrong as her mother.

But the apple may as well be a dildo in my situation, I was that different than my parents. How could I make her understand? That was fine for her because it was what she wanted. Why did I have to want the same thing my parents had?

"You're more upset because you're being told to do it. You don't have to explain," she explained when I opened my mouth, prepared to argue. "I know. Nobody wants to be told what to do. But this isn't worth fracturing the family over. I know I've never been very hard on you, but I think your father is right. You need a little bit of responsibility to settle you down. No one is asking you to work full-time for the company. This is only a single project. Who knows? Maybe you'll end up enjoying it."

What a shame I wanted to puke over the idea of giving Dad what he wanted. Essentially admitting I'd been a fuckup to that point, but there was nothing a little hard work couldn't cure. Sanctimonious bullshit.

The only thing I could imagine enjoying was the chance to spend a little time with the untouchable Rose Goldsmith, who had only grown hotter as the years had passed. That wasn't exactly something I could share with my mother, so instead, I forced the closest thing to an agreeable smile as I could. It made my jaw ache like hell. "I'll do it, and I won't complain. But don't expect me to have this sudden change of heart where I realize I enjoy getting my hands dirty."

Her lips twitched, and her eyes twinkled as she patted my cheek again. "Believe me, honey. I'm an optimist. I'm not delusional."

I was no closer to understanding my father's rhetoric by the time I arrived in East Hampton. It wasn't yet nine in the morning on a quiet Sunday.

My day was normally ending, not beginning. Many Sunday mornings, I'd be stumbling into my apartment around this time. But no, I'd already endured a few rounds with my old man and battled traffic on Route 495.

This was the kind of person my father wanted me to become. The early bird catching the worm or some shit. What did people get out of waking up early and hitting the ground running? Self-satisfaction? How the hell far could that possibly get them? Or was it all for show, the way I imagined this meeting had to be?

There I was, figuring we would meet up sometime in the afternoon, maybe grab an early dinner. But no, that wasn't good enough for Rose.

I didn't expect her to be around when I arrived. I figured

this was one giant pissing contest, her way of reminding me who was boss. She had set the time, but she would show up when she felt like it for the sake of proving a point. Instead of finding the location dark and empty when I arrived, I pulled my Bugatti in beside a fire-red Mustang, the only other car parked in the small lot behind the building.

By the next morning, it would be full of equipment. This was the calm before the storm.

The back door was propped open with a brick placed in front of the door to keep it that way. I wasn't sure what to expect when I stepped inside, lifting my sunglasses and peering into the near darkness.

There she was, framed by the store's front windows. The windows were covered with white paper, which blocked everything but the brightest rays of the sun from filtering into the space. It turned her figure into nothing more than a silhouette against a stark white backdrop. Because of that, I couldn't get a read on her expression when she heard my footsteps and whirled around.

"Oh," she breathed out, going still.

I waited for more, but the wait was in vain. "That's all you have to say?" I prompted without bothering to hide my smug satisfaction. There was no such thing as a translation guide when it came to Rose, but I didn't need one. It was far too easy to see through her.

"Didn't expect me to show up on time?" I asked, taking my phone from my pocket and tapping the screen. "Looks like I'm five minutes early." I held the device out to prove myself.

Eventually, she stopped sputtering long enough to retort, "I didn't hear you come in. That's all. Don't put words into my mouth." She was still deep in shadow, but I would have bet anything her cheeks were tomato red. That was one thing about her I remembered from when we were kids. She blushed at the drop of a hat, never more so than when she was caught lying.

"Trust me." I began walking around, examining the brick walls but still keeping her in the periphery of my vision. "If I'm going to put something in your mouth, it won't be words." She stiffened but didn't make a sound. "So this is it, huh?" I asked, impressed.

The stately structure had once been a bank before its conversion to a bookstore. It had retained its old-school charm thanks to crown molding, elaborate plasterwork, exposed brick, and gorgeous hardwood floors.

"This is it. In four weeks, it will be a high-end boutique." Rose slid her hands into the back pockets of her jeans, turning in a slow circle as she surveyed the interior. The wonder etched across her face did nothing to soften my resentment at being dragged out here, but I couldn't stop watching her.

"You see it in your head, don't you?" I asked.

"Sure. That's the only way to make something come true. You have to see it in your head first. Crystal clear, down to the last detail." She stopped and tipped her head to the side, looking at me as if for the first time. "Don't you do that?"

She saw me. I didn't want to be seen, especially when she also had a talent for making me feel small like there was something wrong with me because I didn't possess her insane work ethic.

"Not unless we're talking about imagining a three-way with a pair of Italian models. That, I get crystal clear." I paired my comment with a wink that made her groan.

"Why am I not surprised?" She folded her arms and narrowed her emerald eyes. "You know what you're doing around here? You're sure about this?"

This again. The woman was determined to shred what was left of my patience, which was already in short supply. "Let's get one thing straight. I wouldn't insult you by pretending I asked to be put in this position." Running my hand over one of the four marble and plaster pillars that formed a large rectangle in the center of the floor, I said, "I did more during my internships than fuck around all day. I'm not going into this blind."

"What if I told you I want to get rid of these pillars?" Standing diagonally from where I stood, Rose ran a hand over the plasterwork and shook her head. "It breaks up the flow of the room. I want this to be as open as possible. We are prioritizing sight lines, and these monstrosities are getting in the way. Literally."

"Why not hold up a sign saying *this is a test*?" I asked before yawning. I'd expected something more challenging than this. "For one thing, they're load-bearing, and you know as well as I do there are guidelines we need to work around if we're going to preserve the structure's architectural touches. One of those lovely little sticking points you agreed to when you purchased the building and received approval from the village council."

Her lips twitched before she turned her face away like she was looking at something else rather than hiding her grin. "Okay. You can't blame me for being curious."

"You say curious. I say cynical," I countered. "I'm more than just a pretty face."

"Are you more than that?" She arched an eyebrow, smirking. "I'm not sure yet."

"But you do admit I have a pretty face?"

Her cheeks flushed before her lashes fluttered, and she looked away again, breaking the moment. Clearing her throat, she walked to the long table in front of the window, then flipped a nearby switch, illuminating a pair of work lights trained on the table's surface. "You're definitely not suffering from a lack of self-esteem. Not that you ever did," she added.

"It could be worse," I reminded her as she unrolled blueprints across the table. "I could be some narcissistic prick who acts like he's God's gift with nothing to back it up."

"And you've got plenty to back it up, is that it?" She looked me up and down, her gaze softening. "I mean, I've heard plenty, but I know better than to listen to gossip." Her lips parted, inviting my attention.

That pink lip gloss would look good ringing my dick.

"I forgot what a smart girl you are." Because she might've been somebody else's woman, but I'd be damned if I could deny what instinct demanded. Inching closer, I murmured, "I'd be more than glad to give you a little firsthand experience if you're interested."

When she leaned close enough that our bodies brushed and the air practically crackled around us, I knew I had won.

That was until her eyes went hard. Jaw clenched, she returned her attention to the blueprints. Hot and cold, back and forth. Who did she think she was kidding, putting on this frigid act? "I'm a smart girl. Too smart for this," she grunted out. "Shall we continue looking around?"

"That's what we're here for," I agreed.

I had never once asked a woman I was about to fuck whether or not she was involved with another man. The way I saw it, he wasn't doing his job properly if she was out sniffing for fresh dick. It wasn't my problem. This was different. I was the one in pursuit, wishing she would stop fighting herself. She was too. It couldn't have been more obvious.

But it had to end.

I didn't go around trolling for pussy.

It came to me.

I wasn't about to beg.

Besides, she was all about relationships. I was only looking for a good time, a way to make a miserable fucking situation slightly more bearable.

"Obviously, I want this to have a different look and feel from the flagship store." She unrolled a design rendering for me to check out, spreading it over the table. The work lights revealed familiar handwriting here and there, indicating different design elements.

"This is something my mom did," I murmured, noting the soft colors and the use of light to create warmth. "Isn't it?"

"I couldn't turn down my mom when Lourde offered to do the interior." She bit her lip, looking my way. "Do you think that was the right choice?"

For someone with all this self-confidence, she didn't seem too sure of herself. Was it an act? "No, they know their business," I assured her, which somehow made it possible for her to release a soft sigh. Relief? Over my opinion? No, I had to be imagining things. The lack of sleep probably had my head fucked up.

Or it could have been her nearness and the perfume she wore. It was slightly spicy, something I couldn't quite identify but would have loved to spend time familiarizing myself with. Hours, preferably, just the two of us...

She cleared her throat, and I realized I was staring like some drooling imbecile "It's going to be a great store," I announced. "You'll do quite well around here. Plenty of women with nothing but time and money on their hands. The money might as well go to you."

She paused in the middle of rolling the renderings. "Wow. Sound more dismissive, why don't you."

"Did I?" I asked before barely stifling a yawn. "It's the truth."

"Is that what you think this is about?" Forgetting the papers, she turned to me with her hands on her hips. "You think we cater to bored women with nothing better to do than throw money around?"

"Calm down." I sighed. "I was talking about them. Not you. There's a difference."

Her head snapped back, and the temperature in the room dropped a few degrees. "I shouldn't be surprised. Respecting women has never been one of your strong points."

"Oh, for fuck's sake." She was giving me a headache with her holier-than-thou shit. "Are you going to be this uptight for four weeks? Remind me to bring a flask to get through it." Before she could say a word, I held up my hands. "It looks like it's going to be a fairly smooth renovation. I'm going to go find a way to make my old man pay for putting me up to this."

I was halfway to the door before her light footsteps rang out behind me. "Wait. I said *wait!*" Her almost shrill cry echoed in the empty space, causing me to stop without turning to face her. "I just want this to go well, okay? But I won't have you insulting our clients."

"I don't work for you," I reminded her.

"Still. They deserve respect. And so do I," she added. "If that makes me a pain in the ass... well, so be it. But I really need this to work. Okay?"

I wasn't leaving because she was a pain in the ass. I was leaving because if I didn't, I would end up doing something I couldn't take back, like kissing her until she forgot her name if only to shut her up.

And I needed this to work too. I needed a success under my belt before telling Dad he could get fucked if he thought I'd turn this into a full-time job.

But I couldn't stop wanting her.

"It's better that I go now, anyway." I continued to the back door, and she followed until we emerged into the bright sunshine. Lowering my sunglasses, I walked to my car, prepared to make my getaway.

"Just give me a second, would you? I don't want things to go this way." Anxiety rang out in her words, and I looked over my shoulder to find her chewing her lip hard enough that it had to hurt.

"Neither do I," I growled out. "But that doesn't mean I'm hanging around, hoping to get kicked in the balls."

"I don't want to..." Anything Rose was about to say died. She went silent, so suddenly I turned around, wondering what was wrong. I found her blinking rapidly, staring past me.

All at once, everything changed. She rolled her shoulders back, lifted her chin, and pasted on a brilliant smile. "Landon! Hi!"

I needed to see who the hell had inspired this sudden one-eighty. Even her voice changed. Now, it was sunny, upbeat, almost bubbly.

I looked over my shoulder, scanning the sidewalk beyond the lot, and I had to grind my teeth to hold back a laugh. Landon motherfucking Jones. I hadn't seen him in at least a year, though I'd heard a lot about him recently. He wanted to be a big-shot politician.

All I saw when I looked at him was the little shit back in prep school, bragging about his father being a judge and how it meant he could get away with whatever he wanted. Not even I said things like that, and everybody knew money could buy just about anything. That was never something we were short on in my family.

"Will you excuse me?" Rose looked like she wished I were absolutely anywhere else but in front of her. "I need to go speak to Landon. I'll see you tomorrow."

I should have been the bigger person and done what she asked.

But I had never much liked doing what I was supposed to do.

That was why I lifted a hand overhead. "Landon! How's it going?" I called out, pretending to ignore Rose's miserable groan behind me.

Landon waved in recognition, then crossed the street rather than head inside the café, where Rose had spotted him. "Do me a favor," Rose whispered fiercely at my back. "Just keep out of this, will you? If you never do anything else for me, please do this. I'll owe you."

Now, I was especially glad to be around while this unfolded. I couldn't imagine what she wanted to do with a stiff like Landon. My curiosity knew no bounds as I watched Rose walk around my car so she could cut Landon off before he reached me.

He was the picture of a bland political candidate in his khakis and a pale blue button-down peeking out from beneath a navy sweater like he'd been forced out of a cookie press.

It didn't seem to matter to Rose. "I was just thinking about you," she told him, rocking from her heels to the balls of her feet and back again. She tucked her hair behind her ears before smiling up at him. "I wanted to congratulate you on your announcement."

"Oh, thanks. It's been a whirlwind, you know?" His attention turned my way when I approached, and his smile widened as he outstretched a hand. "Colton. Long time, no see."

"Too long," I agreed with a laugh that felt more genuine when Landon's gaze bounced from me to Rose and back again. He was already interested in us being out here together. "What's this about you running for state senate? I guess they'll let anybody do that nowadays, huh?"

He laughed along with me. "And what about you? I didn't think you had time for nice girls like Rose." He was trying to undercut me, making me look like shit so he'd look better by comparison. After laughing at his pathetic joke, he shrugged. "I don't know. There are plenty of people who think I've got a chance, so I figured what the hell." I enjoyed the way he tried to laugh it off, as if he had no ambition of his own, and like I couldn't see the wheels turning in his head. "Listen, we're going to have our first fundraiser this week here at my dad's place. I'd better see you there. I need my old crew to represent." Landon flashed a wide toothy grin worthy of an Oscar.

Fucking snake.

"I wouldn't miss it." I probably would. I didn't give a shit about politics and fundraisers. The only reason he wanted me there was to beg for money. And given our history, I had no doubt he would think of it as a victory, having me on the guest list.

He always did have a thing for comparing us. I could count at least five girls off the top of my head who he'd fucked after I had but didn't give a shit about before. If I got a new car, he had to get a newer one. If he told people about the car, it was always in comparison to the model I happened to drive. He was about as difficult to see through as a piece of plastic wrap.

And Rose was looking up at him like he was fucking Superman with a ten-inch cock. Now, I wasn't so flattered by her wanting me, knowing she wanted this bland piece of nothing too.

"I've been in the area a lot more now that we're working on the new store," she told him. "Maybe we could get together for coffee sometime? Talk about your campaign?"

He shrugged amiably. "Sure. You have my number, right?" Before she could reply, he reached into his pocket and withdrew a business card for her, then handed one to me—*Landon Jones for State Senate*. "I'd better go. Dad's across the street, and he hates to be kept waiting. I'll have the invite hand-delivered to you!"

"I'll be working on Rose's new store," I called out as he retreated. For some reason, I needed him to know I'd be around. "Have it delivered here."

I watched Landon jog across the street, lifting his hand to an approaching driver as he did. He shook hands with an older woman coming out of the café after holding the door for her, and they exchanged a few seconds of pleasant conversation before he headed inside. Definitely a politician.

Long after he disappeared, Rose stood with her back to me. Almost like she knew what she was in for. "Let me get this straight," I prompted, staring at the back of her blonde head while flipping Landon's business card in my hand. "You tell me you're seeing somebody, and that's why I need to keep my hands off you, but then I watch you practically stand on your head to get Landon's attention. You even asked him out for coffee. Exactly how attached are you to this guy you're dating that you can throw yourself at Landon?"

"You couldn't have done me *one* favor, could you?" Her shoulders fell before she slowly turned, and the look of pure resentment she wore would've made me laugh if I wasn't confused. Rose didn't strike me as the type to screw around on a boyfriend. If she was, why the fuck would she choose Landon Jones over me?

"He's about as exciting as a decaf latte," I snapped. She opened her mouth, ready to argue, but I shook my head. "No way. You're not changing the subject. I want to know. Are you dating someone, or was that an excuse to get me off you? Because you sure as hell aren't dating Landon Jones from the looks of it. So, which is it?"

6

ROSE

Throughout history, most big moments probably came down to a second here or there.

If a batter swung a split second earlier or later, there would be no home run. If a driver decided to beat the red light, they could cause an accident. Somebody could hit snooze one time too many and inadvertently show up for work late on the day their boss was going to offer them a raise.

I had just gone through one of those moments. And I had made the wrong decision. But then nobody knows at the time when a seemingly meaningless, low-stakes decision will turn out to be pivotal.

I should have let him go. I should not have followed him outside. He was bound and determined to get in his car and drive off like a petulant little brat, and I had stopped him. Because of that, we had crossed paths with Landon.

Now, my lies were coming back to haunt me. What a shame Colton wasn't the kind of person to let things go.

"I have nowhere else to be right now." He didn't bother hiding his judgment, scowling at me like Noah sometimes did. Like he was my protective older brother when the man was anything but.

I rolled my eyes as I nudged my way around him, intending to go back into the building and grab my purse. "I don't owe you an explanation."

"Are you cheating on your boyfriend? Because I'll tell you..." Colton drawled suggestively as he followed me inside. "I could show you a much better time than Landon could ever imagine. The way I heard it, he's never met a woman he couldn't disappoint."

"I didn't know you were acquainted." I made a big deal of slinging my purse over one shoulder, accidentally on purpose, letting it smack Colton before digging around inside like I was looking for something. Anything, so long as I didn't have to look at him.

I could have died of embarrassment. It was one thing to get caught in a lie, but something like this?

"We went to school together," he informed me. "What about you? Are you hoping to become better acquainted with him?"

God, I hated him. "You're having a lot of fun with this, aren't you?"

"I'm not. Because the way I see it, I witnessed you trying to get into Landon's pants when you're already spoken for, or that was a dumb excuse you offered a couple of days ago." He raised his sunglasses once again, folding his arms. He thought he had me cornered.

"Maybe I wouldn't have had to come out and say that if you could've taken no for an answer," I pointed out.

"It *was* a lie," he scoffed, looking incredulous.

"Not exactly. Just listen," I insisted. Of all people to hold themselves in superiority over me. What a joke. "I was thinking of Landon when I told you I was involved with somebody. Really. It was Landon I had in mind."

"You've lost me."

"I don't know how much clearer I can make it. I'm interested in Landon. I want to date Landon." Not half as much as I wanted to die, having to admit all of this to Colton.

His head snapped back while his lip curled in a sneer. "Why?"

"Could you not sound so disgusted?"

"I'm not disgusted," he growled out. "I'm fucking baffled."

"What is there to be baffled about? He's Landon Jones. He's gorgeous, ambitious, and running for state senate, and with his family's connections, there's no way he'll lose. He's on the road to big things and is exactly the kind of man I want in my life."

That did it. That took some of the wind out of his sails. I wanted to be glad about that. He deserved to get taken down a peg or two, as arrogant as he was. Somebody needed to be the one to tell him he wasn't marriage material. A good time, but not much else.

I sort of wished it didn't have to be me when something close to disappointment etched lines across his forehead. "That's a shame, but there's no accounting for taste."

I shrugged and pretended that didn't sting. "You don't need to take it personally. I've been trying to find a way to spend time with him for a while now. I intend to date him."

"Wow. Very romantic. You sound like a robot." He tipped his head to the side, adding, "I guess that would make you a good couple since he's about as interesting as beige paint."

"I'm not asking you to understand. I only ask that you respect my feelings. I am going to date Landon Jones. We are going to be a couple. I only need to grab his attention."

"I hate to tell you, but unless you plan on contributing to his campaign, he won't have much time for you." When I scowled at Colton's snide little prediction, he shrugged. "Consider it a free assessment. Take it or leave it."

"I don't remember asking ... free or otherwise."

"Fine." He spread his arms, backing away while wearing a smirk that made me want to scream. "Waste your time with him. See if I care."

Everybody knew when somebody said that, it meant they cared. Much more than they wanted to let on. But why would he?

"I won't be wasting my time," I retorted. Dear God, why was it so damn important that I prove myself to him? He was the last person on earth whose opinion should have mattered. If anything, I should've taken his disapproval as a great big, flashing green light telling me to go ahead and make Landon mine. The opinion of somebody that lazy and arrogant shouldn't have mattered a bit.

But I couldn't let it go. His arrogant, shit-eating grin was a big part of it. "There's never been anything I've set my mind to in my whole life that I couldn't do."

He went still, dipping his chin and arching an eyebrow, and I knew I'd made a mistake. My first mistake was entertaining his bullshit in the first place. Everything went downhill from there. "I'm not a relationship expert, but I'm pretty sure it doesn't work that way." He paired it with a derisive snort because, of course, he did.

"Oh, give me a break," I snapped. "I know you don't set professional goals, but what about personal ones? You mean to tell me you've never seen somebody and known you had to be with them?"

Another mistake.

When was I going to start thinking before I spoke?

Because now, his full mouth twisted into a smirk that somehow managed to make me grit my teeth and set off a fluttering sensation low in my belly at the same time. It wasn't difficult to figure out how countless women had fallen for his act over the years. I was dangerously close to melting already, and I damn well knew better.

"You mean, have I ever walked into a room, set my eyes on a woman, and known right away I would have her?" He snapped his fingers, and the sudden sound made me flinch, though that wasn't a bad thing. It woke me up and put the brakes on any treacherous pussy moistening that may or may not have been going on. "All the time. Fairly recently, in fact."

I will not show him what he's doing to me.
I. Will. Not.

My nails dug into my palms while I forced myself to take a deep breath. "There you go. What's so different about what I'm doing?"

"For starters, you're talking about seeing somebody and knowing you want to fuck." His bluntness was nails on a chalkboard. "But what you want out of Landon isn't a meaningless hookup. It's a 'relationship.' " The fact that he put air quotes around the word told me all I needed to know about his opinion. "That's what you want with him, right? The white picket fence, the two kids, the dog, and the station wagon." Disdain dripped from his voice. The asshole.

His parents were crazy in love with each other after almost thirty years together. Shouldn't he have known better?

"I want a lot more than that," I muttered.

"That's not the same as seeing somebody and knowing you want to fuck them." He leaned against the nearest pillar, the picture of casual grace. Hot enough to suck the air out of the room and make me wish I didn't know him as well as I did.

I hated how much I wanted him. Enough that it made me hate myself a little. If anything, though, I should have thanked him for putting things into perspective. Wanting to fuck him was a hell of a lot different than wanting to have a life with Landon.

I was even able to genuinely smile before I said, "Thank you for the lesson, Dr. Romance. I'm just fine as is."

"Oh, sure," he muttered with a smirk. "You looked really fine out there when you couldn't get the guy to agree on a coffee date."

Why the hell did he have to be there?

"Fuck off," I muttered before I could help it. "It's not my problem you have a grudge against him."

"Grudge?" He laughed long and hard enough that I regretted saying it. "No, honey. You've got it all wrong. I've never cared enough about him to have a grudge against him." His head fell back before he laughed again. I had never wanted to scream, stomp my feet, and pound somebody with my fists so much.

How did he do it?

How did he make me feel so small?

"What is it then?" I almost shouted to be heard over his laughter. "Landon's got everything. He's got looks, ambition, and connections. He's driven."

He didn't miss a beat. "Then why has he always wanted what I have?"

It was my turn to laugh, and I didn't bother trying to hold back. Why would I want to spare his feelings when he seemed to go out of his way to hurt mine? "I knew you had an ego, but this is pathetic," I managed before laughing again.

He seemed unbothered. "It was a joke with us back at school. I slept with a girl. He slept with that girl. If I dated a girl, he would either wait until I broke up with her, or he would start dating her roommate and compare the girls to each other like he got the better one. Ask Noah if you don't believe me. He'll tell you the same thing."

Right. Like my brother wouldn't back him up no matter what he said. It was part of their bro code, and they talked about it like it was something that should be respected above all else. "So you think he's a loser?"

"Yeah. If you want to boil it down, that's what I think he is." Folding his arms, he flicked his gaze over me. I wish I could say I didn't like it or that a shiver didn't run through me, delicious and a little dangerous. "And I think you're selling yourself short if you think he'll be enough for you," he concluded.

There it was, the most ridiculous assertion of all. "I know what I want. I know what I need. I know who is enough for me. I don't need you making those decisions."

"So you really want to be with the bland, boring guy with the cheesy politician smile, huh? That's your goal in life?"

I held up a finger. "One of my goals. I want a future with someone stable. Landon will give me that."

All at once, his face went slack for a second, barely long enough to be noticeable before he pulled himself together. It helped that I was staring at him, hardly blinking. I couldn't miss the shift in his features. "What?" I ventured.

"You want Landon Jones? I can get you Landon Jones." He stroked his square jaw, and what a shame it seemed like he was laughing at me since he had such a nice, disarming laugh. "I can serve you Landon Jones on a silver platter."

I did not like the sound of that. Rather than trying to

figure him out, I laughed it off. "Right. I'm a little too old for fairy tales."

"Believe me or don't. It's not my problem." He pretended to check his nails but kept shooting me looks from beneath his brows, silently daring me.

I shouldn't have entertained his insanity, but there was no ignoring my curiosity. "You mean to tell me you, of all people, can set me up with Landon?"

"That's right."

"Like you're just going to order him up at the deli?" I asked with a disbelieving laugh while turning the idea over in the back of my mind, wondering if it was possible.

"Says the girl who thinks she can make a boyfriend out of a guy just because she decides that's how she wants it," he countered with a smirk.

Was he serious? How could he be? What I needed to do was tell him to go, that we would meet up in the morning, and ideally, put all of this behind us. At the moment, it didn't matter if I never heard Landon's name again. I wanted this to be over.

I also wanted to know what he thought he could do. "What's your plan? You'll put in a good word for me? And what do I have to do in return? Go out with you? Sleep with you?"

His brows drew together, but he shook his head. "No. You don't have to do that."

He was being entirely too calm and reasonable about this. Suspicions skittered up my spine and made the hair on the back of my neck lift.

Last chance. Get out while you still can.

No way. I had to know what was going on in that handsome head of his. "What would I have to do?"

The corner of his mouth pulled upward. "Pretend. You only have to pretend we're dating."

If anything, I was disappointed. I thought he had more imagination. Landon was supposed to be the boring one. "It is way too early in the day for me to be this tired." I rubbed my temples and shook my head, trying to laugh it off. "Can we pretend none of this ever happened?"

What a surprise. He pretended like I never spoke. "Notice the way he brought up the fundraiser? That he wanted me to be there?"

"Because he wants your money." I sighed.

He waved a hand like it wasn't important. "Obviously. He also wants me there to see how great things are going for him. He's showing off. He'll be the star of the show, and having me there will boost his ego."

"I think your ego is the problem right now." And I was being kind. "He's got it all, but you think he's jealous of you?"

"Have it your way. I could be handing you a shortcut to the man of your dreams. All you have to do is take advantage of this offer." He lifted an eyebrow, challenging me, unlocking every competitive impulse I possessed. "Can you swallow your pride long enough? Do you have it in you to let somebody think you're slumming with Colton Black?"

He was still snickering when I waved my hands and shook my head in a weak attempt to shut this down, no matter how tempting it sounded. "We would never get away with it. Somebody from one of our families would find out, and then we would have to explain it."

"Aren't we working together?" he countered. "So what if we were seen together somewhere? What if we were having dinner with an up-and-coming politician? After all, he's an old friend of mine. Or so he thinks," he snidely added.

He made a point. No one could have been more surprised than I was about it, but he made a point. Landon was an old friend of Colton's from school. Nobody would think twice about us being seen in public at Landon's fundraiser. We could easily explain it away. "But he just saw us out there," I murmured, biting my lip. "And we clearly aren't dating."

"You asked him for coffee to talk about his campaign. That's all. Nothing about that excludes us from being a couple. He's already run into us together," he added as if that helped. "Believe me. He won't give it much thought. All he'll care about is the two of us being together, which will make you much more fuckable in his eyes."

"Wow. You really know how to charm a woman."

He narrowed his eyes like a snake, though a snake might've made me feel safer than he did. "Believe me," he countered in a low voice full of sinful promise. "If I wanted to charm you out of your panties here and now, you wouldn't stand a chance."

It was the perfect time for the final obstacle to occur to me. Otherwise, I might have proven him right. "What am I thinking?" I slapped a trembling hand to my forehead. "Nobody's going to believe we're together. We would never convince him."

He cocked his head to the side before growling. "You don't think so?" Pushing away from the pillar in one smooth movement, he began to advance. His eyes focused on me. All at once, my mouth went dry, and my heart took off like a scared rabbit being chased by a wolf.

In fact, that was what was happening.

"You don't give yourself enough credit," he continued, shaking his head and clicking his tongue in mock sympathy while his eyes pinned me in place. I held my ground as long as I could, but soon, he was too close for comfort. I backed away, afraid to breathe, until my back hit the pillar behind me.

Damn, he was fast. On me in a heartbeat, one arm to either side of my body.

Too close.

Too much.

Could he hear my heart pounding from where he stood?

Somehow, I pulled in enough breath to whisper, "That'll do it. I think you've made your point." It was supposed to come out sounding strong, sure of myself, but it was more like the sound a person makes when they didn't mean a word they were saying.

"Have I?" I went stiff when he leaned closer, so warm and strong. He smelled so damn good, like musk, tobacco, and leather.

The heat from his breath stirred a yearning in me. I knew I wanted him. That was no big surprise.

But this?

This went deeper.

I needed him.

He lowered his head and brushed his lips against my ear, and I shuddered against him. There was no way to fight it. "That's enough," I rasped, squirming a little, hoping to get him to back off. All it did was make my taut nipples brush against his chest, sending a ripple of sensations racing through me. He hadn't laid a finger on me, but that didn't keep my pussy from going hot and wet all at once.

"Maybe we ought to practice," he growled out, letting his cheek brush against mine, light as a feather but hot enough to singe. He moved his head, angling it until our eyes met. I was undone by them and the promise of unspeakable pleasure in those dark depths.

I gave my head the tiniest shake, my gaze darting to his lips and back up again. "I don't think so." Even as I said it, my back arched, my body betraying me. I needed the touch of his body. I needed it even more than I needed him to stop this before it was too late.

"How else could we make it believable? You do want him to believe us, right?" His mouth was inches from mine, our breath mingling between us, and it would have been so easy to lean forward and catch his lips.

Just to see what they tasted like.

Just to see if ten years had improved his technique.

And just like that, my thoughts drifted back to his eighteenth birthday...

There he was, leaning against the balustrade with his arms folded on the stone surface. He hadn't changed out of the charcoal gray slacks and white button-down he'd worn earlier, only now the sleeves were rolled up to his elbows. He stood against the backdrop of twinkling city lights, and a rush of evening breeze stirred his dark hair. The scent of his cologne drifted my way and woke my body up in the worst way.

God, he was cute.

More than anything, it was the way he stood. There was something tired and almost defeated in his posture. That was what made me different from all the other girls. The fact that I could see past what was on the outside.

Instead of backing away and pretending I didn't see him there, I decided to take a chance. "Hey, you. What's on your mind?" I murmured.

The smile he wore once he slowly turned made me tingle to the tips of my toes. He smiled at people he really knew and liked. Not the fake, wide smile he gave most people when he was trying to show off. "There you are," he said. "I was wondering if I was going to see you tonight."

Was that true? It would be a shame if it weren't since my heart was about to burst out of my chest. "Here I am. In my pajamas," I added with a shaky little laugh. *What a disappointment that I had already taken off my makeup and pulled my blonde waves up in a bun.*

"You look cute." *He said it so casually, like it was a fact.*

Still, I cringed, not exactly how I wanted him to see me. "Cute? Thanks."

"Like it's an insult," *he teased with a grin.* "You looked very nice tonight before you got changed. You looked beautiful."

This was it. I was going to fall over the balustrade and drop hundreds of feet to the sidewalk. "You're drunk," *I muttered, rolling my eyes. What a relief it was dark out, so he couldn't see the heat flushing my skin.*

"Dead sober," *he countered.* "I sort of promised to be a good boy tonight. At least during the party." *There was something wicked in his grin, and for the millionth time, I wished I wasn't three years younger, and he would see me as somebody on his level rather than looking at me like I was a kid.*

"Did you have fun?" *That was what I really wanted to know. That was what mattered. Whether he enjoyed his party, I wanted him to be happy more than anything.*

"Sure. Who wouldn't? I haven't even started counting up all the money I got in cards. I might be able to buy myself the Bugatti I've had my eye on," *he joked. When I didn't laugh along with him, his brows knitted together.* "Why? Did it not seem like I was having fun?"

"It's not my job to watch you twenty-four seven." *I rolled my eyes again, and he snickered before I added,* "But honestly? I noticed a few times, and you looked sort of distracted. Even bored."

I shouldn't have said it. The silence that hung over us made me want to crawl back into the penthouse and pretend the whole conversation never happened. When would I ever learn? It probably weirded him out, thinking I was watching him like some stalker.

When the corners of his mouth lifted, my heart lodged in my throat. "How do you do that?" *He moved a little closer, and now my heart was banging wildly against my ribs. I swallowed hard and forced myself to stay where I was rather than running away.*

"Do what?" *I whispered.*

"It's like you see through me. Everybody else sees one thing, but you see... the truth." *He sighed, then lifted his broad shoulders in a shrug.* "I was kind of bored. There were a lot of people around I didn't even know. But I had to pretend and pose for a lot of pictures and shake a lot of hands. It was boring as fuck."

A laugh burst out of me when he said it like that, and he laughed with me. "But isn't it nice to know so many people wanted to be here?" *I asked.*

"Please." *He scoffed and shook his head, taking another step closer. I could almost feel the heat from his body now, and it was driving me insane.* "They weren't here for me. They were here because the powerful Barrett Black invited them."

"I was here for you." *Dammit. Why did it come out like that? It was the truth, but I sounded so childish.*

He didn't seem to think so. "I know you were because you're real," *he murmured. He was so close now, close enough to touch, and there was something different in the way he was looking at me. There had to be something wrong. He had to be drunk. Then again, I couldn't smell it on his breath, and he was breathing right in my face by the time he came to a stop.*

"You know something?" *he asked. I held my breath when Colton reached out to take a strand of my hair between his fingers once the night breeze teased it free from my bun.* "You really did *look beautiful tonight. I would've asked you for a dance back at the hotel, but I kept losing track of you."*

Imagine that, dancing with him in front of all those people. "That's okay," I offered with a shrug. He's only saying this because you're like a sister. Do not get too excited.

There was no stopping it. My heart was about to explode, I couldn't breathe, my legs were shaking, and this was a moment I wanted to exist in forever. When he was looking at me, only me, testing the softness of my hair before tucking it behind my ear, his touch was electric, sending a shiver through me from head to toe.

"What did you get me for my birthday?" It was a whisper meant only for my ears.

"I didn't get you anything," I confessed. "It was like a family gift from all of us. I wouldn't know what to get you, anyway. You have everything."

His head tipped to the side before his eyes narrowed. "I can think of one thing I didn't get tonight."

This was happening.

It was really happening.

But instead of letting me enjoy it, my stupid brain had to fight. "Colton, we shouldn't..."

His breath warmed my already flushed skin. "But do you want to, Rose?" He didn't know my heart was mixed up in this.

"Yes," was all I could whisper back before I leaned up, and his mouth was on mine, and the whole world exploded in bright colors, glitter, and fireworks.

"Tell me something," he whispered. One of his hands landed on my waist, then began sliding down to my hip, closer to the heat threatening to boil over. I had to fight the impulse to part my thighs to make room for him.

How much longer would I be able to hold back? I was almost in over my head, sinking, losing strength.

His fingers pressed against my denim-covered flesh before he whispered, "When was the last time somebody fucked you the way you need to be fucked?"

His question was meant to be seductive. I knew that. But all it did was dump a bucket of ice water over my head, shaking me out of my almost painful arousal and bringing me back to reality. I had almost forgotten exactly who had me pinned against the pillar and exactly why he was entirely the wrong person for me in every way.

"That's none of your business." I sounded a lot more like myself when I grabbed Colton's wrist and pulled his hand off me. "You proved your point. We could be convincing if we had to."

Still, he didn't back away. He was a little breathless himself as if he had forgotten the point he was trying to make and let himself get caught up. I wasn't stupid enough to take that as a compliment. He probably got hard twenty times a day.

"So that's it?" he asked, backing off, and I hated the part of me that was sad when he did.

When was the last time I was good and properly fucked? I had no idea. I couldn't remember. And that was clearly a problem since it made me dangerously vulnerable to certain arrogant jerks. It made me want to throw myself at them, wrap my body around theirs, and climb them like a tree.

I had a hell of a lot of anxiety to burn off.

My head bobbed before I found my full voice. "Yes. That's it. If you think it'll work, I'm willing to play along."

"I'll have somebody reach out to Landon and tell him we will be attending his fundraiser." He looked me up and down before lowering his sunglasses and turning away.

"Make sure you have a nice dress. You'll want to impress him."

So that was what it felt like to make a deal with the devil. I sank against the pillar once the sound of his engine faded, touching my flushed cheek to the cool marble.

I had four weeks of working together ahead of me and had barely made it through three days. Now, we'd have the added fun of a fake relationship to spice things up. "Landon..." I breathed, closing my eyes, "... you had better notice me fast."

Because I had no idea how much longer I could come up with reasons to resist Colton.

7

COLTON

"How's it feel being a working man?" Noah's laughter filtered through the speaker on my phone and filled the bedroom. "Do you have calluses on your fingers yet?"

It was spoken like a guy who sold high-end real estate for a living. For him, a stressful workday involved back-to-back showings of an Upper East Side penthouse. "Working is everything I was always promised it would be." Straightening my bow tie, I muttered, "It makes me wonder how most people get through the fucking day."

"It's that bad? I figured it was kind of a figurehead position. Sit around typing on a laptop, pretend to send a few emails, and make sure everybody knows you're watching." He snickered. "You're goddamn lucky. Rose probably doesn't trust you to handle much."

My reflection scowled at me. "I can handle shit," I reminded him, glancing down at the phone. "I know what I'm doing."

He groaned. "Shit, man. You know I'm fucking with you.

And don't tell me my sister isn't micromanaging every second of the work."

"She is hands-on." Though not as hands-on as I'd expected. I figured she'd be up my ass morning, noon, and night. If anything, the way she'd stepped back was a little disconcerting. As of Sunday, she was a nervous little hummingbird, fluttering around and reminding me of everything she had riding on this.

Since then, we'd barely exchanged a few sentences while this night loomed in front of us. No doubt she felt it too. Every time she'd avoided eye contact or left a room because I entered it, I reminded myself there wouldn't be any way to avoid me tonight. Not when she wanted to impress her beloved Landon.

The fundraiser was set to begin in less than fifteen minutes. "I've got to fuck off now," I told Noah. "Gotta head over and pretend I was ever friends with that spineless little shit, Jones."

"I'm a little bummed you didn't score me an invite." He laughed. "And there I was, thinking we were tight."

"Hell, man. If you're that hard up for an invite, just show up. Offer him a few million. You'd get right in."

"No, I'll let you be my representative," he announced with another laugh. "I'm trusting you tonight."

"Trusting me with what?"

"With my sister. I heard she's got her eye on that walking toothpaste commercial, Landon." I could practically hear him roll his eyes. "Do me a solid and make sure she doesn't end up going too far. You know how she is when she sets her mind on something."

He had no idea how well I knew. "Don't worry about it," I assured him, checking my pockets after sliding into my jacket. "I'll keep her busy enough that she won't be able to do that."

"Okay, don't keep her *too* busy." His knowing chuckle made me pause. "This isn't an excuse to get her drunk and fuck around. She's not one of those girls."

I wasn't sure what made me grind my teeth. That he needed to remind me or that he thought I would take advantage of her. "She's a big girl. She doesn't need to be babysat. I'll try not to get any of my stench on her," I concluded, teeth clenched.

"Fuck." He groaned louder than before. "Work is turning you into a bitch. You know I didn't mean it that way."

I wasn't so sure as we ended the call. The problem with having a friend who knew everything about me was having a friend who knew *everything about me*. It was all fun and games when we were out looking for pussy, but as soon as life got real, I was a piece of shit who wasn't good enough to touch his sister.

I was still grinding my teeth when I pulled away from my family's Hamptons home and headed out to the far end of the island where the Goldsmith estate sat. Rose told me she would be getting ready there when I offered to pick her up. We had to make this couple thing look real, which meant arriving together.

I flexed my hands as I drove, taking turns between them. The truth was, I had done a lot more than banging on a keyboard since Monday. One of the crewmembers' wives went into labor on Tuesday, and his absence meant needing to redistribute some of the day's tasks. I'd ended up working on a table saw for the first time in years, measuring and cutting. It was remarkable how quickly time passed and how much I'd enjoyed getting into the flow of the work. By the time I'd finished, my clothes were covered in sawdust, and my eyes were tired from squinting at the tape measure countless times, but there was something to show for it.

Dad would've been so proud if only he were capable.

My cynical laughter filled the car as I steered it onto the driveway leading up to the main house. Olivia and Ari were married here when I was only a couple of years old. Naturally, I had no memory of that, but countless events had taken place there in the years since.

It was unusual to see it in its normal state. It was still breathtaking, with dramatic lighting and a marble fountain in the center of a circular front courtyard, but without the presence of countless guests and valets.

I sent Rose a text telling her I was waiting, then stepped out of the car to get a breath of air. I'd expected her to be waiting on the front stairs, tapping her foot and pointing at her watch, but then it was just as likely she was anxious and stressed over how she looked. She was wasting her time on him, but I couldn't tell her that. She was too damn stubborn to listen.

After a minute or two of pacing beside the car, I was prepared to head up and ring the doorbell until she came out. One look up the wide staircase told me I didn't have to. She was standing there, waiting at the top, looking down at me.

I forgot how to breathe as her eyes fixed on mine.

This is it. This is how I die. Killed by the sheer presence of a woman.

Not just any woman. A tall, regal blonde whose body was perfectly encased in an elegant red dress that moved softly around her as she began her graceful descent. I would have sworn there was a spotlight trained on her. She seemed to glow.

Her hair shone in its upswept curls. Diamonds sparkled

at her ears and throat. I damn near rocked back on my heels when she reached the landing and came to a stop a few feet from me.

"Do I look okay?" With her arms held out to the sides, she turned slowly. It was a wonder I didn't swallow my tongue when I caught sight of her back. The dress was cut damn near down to her ass, exposing an expanse of creamy skin, begging for my hands to touch.

"It's a real shame," I murmured, shaking my head.

"Oh, my God. What? What's wrong?" She nearly shrieked, and I almost laughed when she started examining herself.

A smart girl but damn gullible.

"It's a shame you would go to all this trouble for the Crown Prince of mediocrity." I opened the passenger door and reached for her hand. "But then again, what am I saying? You got all dressed up for your boyfriend because you wanted to look nice for me tonight."

"You look nice, too, by the way." Her crimson lips pursed like she tasted something sour before she placed her hand in mine. I allowed my thumb to run over her knuckles, guiding her into the vehicle. A breeze brought the scent of something floral and sweet my way, and I closed my eyes, concentrating on the scent before closing the door.

Get it together. Get it the fuck together.

It was a relief, turning my focus toward getting us to the black-tie event in one piece, though the drive was a short one. The Jones family had pulled out all the stops to impress Landon's potential donors. I could see the house from half a mile away, gleaming in the dark.

We waited in a short line of cars until it was our turn. Rather than let the staff member help Rose from the car once I stepped out, I handed him my keys and opened her door myself.

A nervous young woman had slid into the car. A queen stepped out of it. She carried herself in a way that commanded attention, holding her head high. Her smile was easy and natural, nothing nervous or forced. When I tucked her hand in my elbow, she turned that smile on me and forced me to remind myself this was an act. She was putting on a show.

"You look stunning," I whispered, and her eyes widened a fraction, her cheeks turning pink before we started up the pathway leading to the Jones mansion.

It wasn't as large as the Goldsmith estate, but it was impressive, and already guests were spilling out from open doors and chatting on the side patio. Lanterns had been strung up there, and a band played soft, gentle standards. I wouldn't want to offend anybody by playing music from the second half of the twentieth century.

"I wonder where he is." Rose only had eyes for Landon, and more than once, she stood on her tiptoes, trying to see over the heads of the dozens of people hugging, kissing, and drinking champagne. I would need something a little stronger than a pretentious, bubbly drink if I was expected to keep from rolling my eyes or gagging.

"Here." I accepted a pair of flutes and handed her one. "Drink this. Loosen up a little. He'll find us," I predicted, nodding in acknowledgment of a few familiar faces. Older people, probably my grandparents' contemporaries. One of the women looked at the other and muttered something that made them both smile before they turned their attention my way again.

What, were they surprised to see me at a respectable

function? Wondering if Daddy knew I was so far off my leash.

We had yet to step into the house, and I could tell Rose's impatience was beginning to grow, but I needed something a little stronger to bolster myself. I hadn't considered needing to make nice with a bunch of fucking hypocrites who thrived on gossip. Like there was a single family in our rarified world who didn't have dark fucking secrets.

Scotch was more my speed, though I made it a point to sip it judiciously as we meandered our way through the party. Inside, the crowd got thicker, meaning we were getting closer to the man of the hour.

"There is a fuck ton of money in this room," I murmured close to Rose's ear.

She turned her head quickly, so suddenly our mouths almost touched. Her lashes fluttered before she cleared her throat. "I'm telling you he can't lose."

"You are really serious about this, huh?" I found it hard to believe, and not only because we had come a heartbeat from kissing. How could she be so smart and so blind?

"I told you this is what I want." Her eyes widened, and she lifted her hand to someone across the room. And just like that, I was forgotten. "Landon, there you are!"

I gritted my teeth as he approached and noticed how his gaze bounced between Rose and me. "Good evening, you two. So glad you could make it on short notice. Rose, you look gorgeous tonight." He leaned in for a chaste peck on her cheek before pulling back and arching an eyebrow at me. "That all right with you?" he asked, grinning. His way of asking the question he wouldn't dare speak out loud. *Is she taken? Have you claimed her yet?*

"Sure," I replied with a grin. It was a good thing I wasn't holding a champagne flute anymore, or I might have broken the stem. "After all, you're going to have to do a lot of kissing on the campaign trail. Babies, old ladies... the asses of countless donors."

"Colton!" Rose placed a hand against my chest while elbowing me with her other arm, getting me right in the ribs. "I swear, I can't take him anywhere," she told Landon before blowing out an exaggerated sigh.

"It's very nice to see you two together like this," he added, turning to her like something had just occurred to him. "You mentioned something about grabbing coffee soon. I would love to do that. Have your assistant reach out to mine, and we'll see what my schedule will permit. You're going to be in the area for a while, right?"

It was a good thing I was holding onto her, or she might have taken flight. As it was, my hand ached from her squeezing the hell out of it. "Yes, I'll be spending a lot of my time on the new store and staying at the house here," she confirmed.

"We'll get together soon." He gave her another kiss, followed by a pat on my shoulder. And then he was gone, kissing ass somewhere else.

"What did I tell you?" I asked, downing the rest of my drink and slamming the glass on the nearest table. "Come on. I feel like dancing."

"What?"

I ignored Rose's question and the laughter that followed, cutting my way through the crowd on the way out to the patio. I needed some air. There were too many bodies everywhere—too much perfume, aftershave, and hairspray—I could barely breathe.

Landon was going to make his move.

He was almost painfully predictable.

What was worse was the absolute joy radiating from Rose once we reached the dance floor, which had been laid out over the brick patio. There were a handful of couples dancing. Old people dancing to old music was practically a fundraiser staple.

We were the youngest couple out there by at least twenty years as I placed a hand against Rose's smooth back and drew her close.

"I have to admit..." she placed her hand in mine, then laid the other on my shoulder, "... I didn't think it would be that easy." She was downright giddy, her eyes sparkling as we began to sway.

"Let's not get ahead of ourselves." I couldn't help but bring her down to reality for her own sake, if for no other reason. He didn't have the first idea what it meant to be with a woman like Rose. He'd never have the time for her. Never put in the effort to satisfy her. "I wouldn't start picking out wedding china yet. Do people still do that?"

"It's a start," she retorted. "He was way more interested in me when he saw me with you."

Her hand slid up my shoulder until it was cupping the back of my neck. "Maybe we should, I don't know... make things look legit? Get him really good and jealous?"

She would never understand how she was trying my self-control. Her body pressed against mine, swaying along with me to a gentle rhythm, looking and smelling like something out of a dream, so beautiful she made heads turn. The lanterns cast pink, blue, and gold light on us, the colors playing across her perfect face.

Hunger uncoiled in my core. What was I doing? Pushing her into another man's arms when I wanted her in my bed tonight. She was buzzed after a couple of glasses of champagne, paired with feeling victorious and practically begging me to take advantage of the situation, pulling me down, seeking my lips.

It would be simple to give in.

She would forget Landon existed.

For once, I wasn't going to let my impulses rule my actions. "We should try to keep it as safe as possible. Remember, there are plenty of people here who know our families." As it was, we were dancing too close, though I would be damned if I let her go. Not yet. I wanted to soak in every moment, knowing the clock was ticking. She'd drop our act the second Landon made prolonged eye contact.

Her mouth fell open slightly before she nodded, tightening her jaw. "You're right, of course. I don't need any middle-of-the-night phone calls from Mom and Dad."

That wasn't enough to keep us from dancing. We stayed on the floor through three songs until a speech from Landon brought everybody into the house.

Except, I didn't hear a word of it.

How could I when I was so deeply interested in the woman holding onto my arm while gazing adoringly at a man who would never be as interested in her as he was in himself?

8

ROSE

What a night. Everything went perfectly. Landon had noticed me. He had remembered my offer to go for coffee. He was interested, finally, and all I had to do was capitalize on that interest.

For once, Colton had come through.

Knowing him, he would never let me live it down.

"I think we did our job." He was moody by the time an hour had passed, not that I expected much else. Obviously, he had a chip on his shoulder about Landon. What a shock. He didn't like somebody who was basically the opposite of him.

I gritted my teeth in something close to a smile, looking up into his arrogant face. "But we've only been here an hour. Doesn't that look shitty, walking out early?"

"And when did I give you the idea I care about looking shitty?" He had a point there. "We got what we came for. I'm sick of hanging around here, making nice. Doesn't the hypocrisy get to you?"

He had a point there too. It *was* a little too ass-kissy around here.

With a smirk, he added, "Though if you would like to stick around and make sure Landon is extra jealous, we can negotiate."

I couldn't get a read on him. He turned me down on the dance floor, which was probably for the best, but now he wanted to flirt. Maybe he was right, and it would be better if we were apart for the rest of the night.

We were halfway to the front courtyard to pick up his car by the time I started going through tomorrow's agenda in my head. It was a habit. And in this case, it was also a necessary distraction. It didn't matter how wrong Colton was for me in every conceivable way. Sometimes, it mattered more that a man looked like sex on two legs in a tuxedo, especially if the man happened to have once occupied a big part of my heart.

If he had gone in for a kiss on the dance floor, I would've kissed him back. And I would have meant it, and that was scary. Dangerous. I was supposed to be in this for Landon, wasn't I?

"Oh, shit. I totally forgot." Checking my phone, I confirmed the meeting scheduled in the morning. "I'm supposed to be meeting with our moms first thing over brunch to discuss a few design changes, but I left them at the store. Can we swing by there on the way home?"

"Do I have chauffeur stamped on my forehead?" he grumbled, rolling his eyes, but he sighed in the end. "Make it fast. I would like to salvage some of this night, if possible."

It shouldn't have bothered me to know he was going out after dropping me off at home. Why did I suddenly feel hot and bitter inside? Let him go out, get wasted, screw a handful of strangers. So long as he showed up to work.

We passed the ride to the store in silence. I would have

thanked him if he didn't insist on being such a dick, from hot to cold with no warning, infuriatingly unpredictable.

"You don't have to come with me," I insisted when he cut the engine once he parked at the curb. "I'll be in and out."

"I love it when you say dirty shit like that." His snide chuckles followed me across the sidewalk and up to the front door, which I unlocked before turning off the alarm.

The sweet smell of freshly cut wood filled the air, and I couldn't help grinning. We would keep a decorative façade mounted on the building's exterior to make it look like the window casements were original to the structure. Still, the truth was the originals needed to be replaced after sneaky termites had destroyed a lot of the wood. That was a big part of the first phase which would be completed by week's end.

"I know they're around here somewhere." It wasn't like I drank a lot at the party, but for some reason, I was unsteady on my feet, fumbling around. The far back corner of the floor would be closed off and used as an office, but for now, there was nothing but a few tables and chairs for Colton and anyone else who needed to use them.

"Take your time," he muttered as I went through the materials. "I have all night."

"Relax," I snapped. Apparently, I wasn't allowed to have a good night. "I'm sure there are still plenty of skanks in dark corners just waiting for you to bless them with your presence."

"Sure." His slow grin was both infuriating and wildly sexy. Hot enough to steal my breath. "But I'm afraid all the good ones will be taken already."

"You have standards now?" Where the hell were the most recent designs? "You know, you could help me with this instead of complaining," I muttered, bunching my dress around my knees before kneeling to look for the folio under one of the tables.

"Oh, now this I like." I wasn't fast enough to get up before his footsteps rang out behind me. "Just like that, baby. Ass in the air."

"Fuck off." I stood, brushing off my knees and dropping my hem. I was only ever going to be a joke to him.

When would I learn?

What a shame I couldn't force my body to stop responding to him like it did.

Right now, for instance, when I turned to find him standing so close, I doubted a whisper could pass between our bodies. Suddenly, there was a wall in front of me—warm, firm, and unyielding—that smelled like want. Desire.

His already dark eyes appeared nearly black by the time he whispered, "I think you need to ease all that tension."

I sucked in a gasp when the faintest touch ran up my spine. His fingers barely skimmed my skin before making the return journey south. I parted my lips so I could breathe, and his gaze landed on them, his eyes half-lidded as he watched me take one short breath after another, studying my reaction.

He wasn't wrong. I did need relief, but not from him. I didn't want to regret anything, and I could only regret being with him. "Wh-what do you think you're doing?" I choked out.

"What does it feel like?" Holy fuck, he was seductive, his voice a deep growl that made my juices flow.

"You shouldn't touch me," I warned in a whisper.

He didn't seem to care, and neither did my ass once his hand slid over it. Oh my God. I was on fire and had barely done anything. "Let me take care of that for you, boss," he growled out.

Suddenly, I was backed against the table, spreading my thighs for him. He was everywhere, all over me, his hands trailing slowly up my calves, taking the dress with them before moving up my thighs. Every inch his skillful fingers covered took me an inch closer to oblivion, and maybe it was knowing how wrong it was that made it feel so right. Knowing it could never happen again.

It shouldn't happen now.

Instinct screamed at me to put an end to it before we went any further. I had to be stronger than this and Colton's hold over me.

Then his fingertips teased my inner thigh, and my strength melted away.

It would only happen once.

Just one time because he didn't do long-term.

It would be fine, so long as I didn't go into it with any expectations. I could handle it. I'd probably hate myself, but I could handle it.

Amazing, the things we could tell ourselves when we were horny as hell and dying to come.

"Like silk," he murmured, leaning over me, teasing me with the idea of a kiss but never quite delivering. He overwhelmed me until I leaned back on my elbows, letting my head drop back when his hot breath fanned across my throat.

Kiss me, just kiss me. I didn't have the nerve to say it. I settled for sighing, bending my legs and pulling him closer to my aching pussy.

"Are you just as silky down here?" When he cupped my lace-covered mound, I lost myself, grinding my hips helplessly.

It didn't matter. He would forget all about it, wouldn't he? This was nothing but a joke.

"I knew it," he growled out, peeling the soaked fabric away from my skin and pulling it down my legs. "All it takes is the right touch, and you're purring like a kitten."

I wanted to tell him to shut up, but all that came out was a long, guttural moan when one, then two of his thick digits stretched my pussy. "Oh my God!" I cried out, angling my hips so he could go deeper. "Colton, fuck!"

"You're so tight," he breathed out, pumping in and out of my drenched hole, teasing my clit with his thumb and driving me insane. Was it possible to die from pleasure? I couldn't handle all the sensations hitting me from all sides.

It was too much.

It wasn't enough.

I opened my eyes and found him staring down at me, breathing hard, consumed by the sight of me. "I'm gonna come," I whispered, working against him, practically humping his hand until the delicious tension broke and I shattered, falling apart while he continued working my sensitive flesh.

Not so sensitive that I didn't whimper in disappointment when he withdrew his fingers. My surprised gasp filled the air as I watched him insert those fingers into his mouth, staring down at me while he licked my juices from his skin.

"Not enough, boss." All at once, he dropped and hooked his arms under my legs, holding them in place. He spread them wide so he could dive between them and lap up what still ran out of me.

"Shit! Oh my God!" I reached out blindly, grabbing the back of his head and holding him close because, yes, this was what I wanted—hearing his animal grunts, the feeling of his tongue parting my bare lips, invading me, claiming me, and bringing out every dark, primal instinct I possessed. He worked my clit with his tongue until I screamed again, my voice went hoarse, and there was nothing to do but lie back across the table in complete exhaustion while my body trembled in the aftermath.

"Mm..." He chuckled darkly, running his lips over the insides of my thighs before he stood. I lifted my head and looked him in the eye, prepared for whatever came next. I wanted everything. No holding back now that we had started.

The sight of my thong landing on my stomach put a stop to all of that. "Let's go," he said before heading to one of the other tables and pulling a leather folio embossed with the name of Mom's company on the front. "The night is still young."

He knew where it was the entire time, the bastard.

I couldn't bring myself to care much, lying there on a table after the most intense orgasm of my life.

It was only a matter of time, wasn't it, until I broke down and gave in to him?

Now, it was only a matter of why the hell he didn't want to keep going. I didn't have it in me to ask. I could only stand and cram my panties into my purse before striding across the store with all the dignity I could muster.

While pretending not to notice his satisfied smirk.

9

COLTON

Work had shown me one thing if nothing else. I could understand better than ever why people looked forward to Friday. I had never looked forward to the weekend this much when I was in school, but then, I'd never worked very hard in school.

I worked my ass off this week, for sure, and not only filling in for a missing crew member or placing phone calls to suppliers dragging their asses instead of delivering what they'd promised. It probably helped that my last name happened to be Black, the same as the company's owner. Regardless of the reason, I got shit done.

That wasn't all I'd spent energy on. Ever since the fundraiser, I'd been ducking Rose like my life depended on it. She was a relationship kind of girl.

What was I supposed to say? You have the most delicious pussy I've ever tasted, but your brother would cut off my balls if he ever knew? Or maybe, the whole thing started as a joke, but before I knew it, my tongue was halfway up your cunt?

It was a real change of pace, in other words. Rose was

the one trying to corner me, trying to get a word in, while I kept myself busy to avoid being alone with her. It was easier that way. She would get the hint. Besides, she had Landon on her plate, and there was way too much fresh pussy in Manhattan for me to get tied down to one in East Hampton.

"What the hell, man?" My cousin, Lucian, checked his phone, laughing as he held it up to display the time. He had the same laugh as his old man, Uncle Connor—throaty and loud. "That's the third time you've yawned in five minutes. Are we that fucking boring?"

I had to raise my voice over the dull roar around us. "In a word? Fuck, yeah." I laughed along with everybody else but was irritated at being so easy to read.

It was a typical Friday night in Midtown, with bodies pressing on all sides and no shortage of eye candy to stir my interest and my dick. If only I weren't so beat after spending a week waking up earlier than I sometimes went to bed, then working nine or ten hours.

"Remember, everybody…" Noah held up his hands, signaling for quiet even as he smirked like the smug prick he could sometimes be, "… our friend, Colton, is getting used to the working man's lifestyle. He's not used to busting his ass all day, then partying all night."

"I'd tell you you'd get used to it, but you won't be doing it long enough," Evan offered with the same easygoing shrug I'd seen a million times since we met on the first day of school.

"Thanks for the encouragement." I set my glass down on the table before slouching in my chair and blowing out a sigh. "It's been a long week."

"I bet my sister didn't make it any easier on you," Noah pointed out with a grimace as if he understood. "She's been busting my balls all my life, so I feel for you."

"She hasn't been that bad." *Why did I defend her?* "She's been in meetings and shit, anyway."

"I bet she works real hard, too," Lucian mused. He wasn't looking at me, though. His attention was somewhere else across the room. I figured he must've landed on tonight's piece of ass.

"Yeah, I guess she does," I agreed with a shrug.

"She doesn't look half as tired as you do." He snorted with laughter before nodding toward where he'd been staring.

What the fuck?

How had I missed her? How was everyone in that packed club not staring at her when she glowed the way she did? She flipped her blonde hair back, laughing, and I'd never wanted anything more than to be the man who made her laugh.

What would I have to do to make her laugh like that for me?

As it turned out, it wasn't a man who made her laugh. "Oh, fuck," I muttered when I recognized my little sister, Sienna, at Rose's side. Not that I didn't want to see her. I didn't feel like getting cock blocked was all. She had a way of fucking with my game like an annoying little sister. What a shame we were too old for that kind of shit.

"Hey, Sienna!" Evan raised an arm overhead because he knew what a pain in the ass it was to run into my sister while I was out with the guys.

Still, I stood, offering her a quick hug when she tottered over on her mile-high heels, arms outstretched. "Don't worry," Sienna told me, almost screaming in my ear to be heard. "I won't make it look like we're together, so you miss out on prime pussy."

"Fuck you," I growled out, making her laugh.

I had inherited Dad's looks, but she was practically Mom's twin. Looking over her shoulder, I caught a pair of dickheads staring at her ass. When they caught me glaring at them, they got real busy looking anywhere else but at my sister.

She looked around the group, holding up her martini glass. "Don't worry, boys. We won't bother you for long. Just trying to be polite."

Lucian arched an eyebrow. "Is that something you PR reps specialize in? Pretending like you're happy to see the people you're air-kissing?"

"One, I'm a PR *specialist*, cousin…" she thrust a hand on her bony hip, "… two, I don't bother with air-kissing." She made it a point to kiss his cheek hard enough to leave lipstick behind.

"What about me?" Evan pointed to his jaw. "We're not related, but doesn't a longtime friend count?" Laughing, she slung an arm around his neck and pressed a smacking kiss against his cheek. I narrowed my eyes at him, but he brushed it off.

"I don't need a kiss," Noah insisted when she looked his way.

Sienna narrowed her eyes. "I wouldn't put my lips anywhere near anything you have, thanks. I've heard too many stories." She pretended to gag while the rest of us laughed. Rather, everyone but Noah, who scowled, his nostrils flaring.

It was always this way. Get us together, and we turned into kids, no matter where we were. All we needed were the twins, Valentina and Aria, and it would be Christmas break all over again, busting balls and pranking.

Only we weren't kids anymore. Now we did things like go down on each other in our place of work.

Their joking faded into the background when my eyes brushed over Rose standing off to the side and laughing at her brother after a much quieter greeting than the one my sister offered.

She had to feel me staring at her. She couldn't resist the brief shifting of her gaze, hitting me before darting away again. She was pissy. She might even have hated me for turning cold. It was for the best. It was Landon she wanted —a relationship and a family. We would only waste each other's time in the end.

But I would be damned if I could keep my eyes off her once she and Sienna peeled off and did their own thing. All my focus, my entire existence, narrowed down until there was nothing but her. Rose's golden head moved through the crowd, bobbing up and down as she walked until they reached the bar at the far end of the long room.

"We good here?" I asked, gesturing toward our drinks. "I was gonna grab the waitress for another round."

"Just don't grab her so hard you forget what you got up for," Noah advised. I left them laughing, determined to... what? I didn't know for sure. I only knew I couldn't sit still while she was there, practically begging to be fucked in a short, black dress that hugged every inch of her luscious curves.

My sister waved at a group of girls then hurried over to them, leaving Rose on her own for the moment.

When a tall, frat-boy-looking douchebag sidled up to her at the bar the second she was alone, I knew I made the right decision by following her. Everything around me went red as my awareness expanded to include this soon-to-be corpse, along with the woman he'd made the mistake of approaching. No way was I going to let him claim what I had already tasted.

I tapped him on the shoulder until he turned away from her. "You're too late. Move on."

"Wait a second!" It didn't matter what Rose said. He huffed but got the message and fucked off without another look her way.

"I wasn't lying," I told her when she slammed her wine glass on the bar before almost snarling at me. "He was too late. You're already in love with Landon, right?"

"After two days, this is how you... no, you know what?" She threw her hands into the air. "Never mind. You ruined my night, thank you very much. I can't even talk to somebody without you being an asshole."

Before she could get past me, my hand closed around her arm. I held her in place, leaning down until my lips brushed her ear. "What if I said he was too late because I already know what that pussy tastes like?"

There was a moment, the length of a blink, when she leaned into me. It was almost like her legs threatened to go out when she remembered the way I made them shake. But just like that, it ended, and she yanked her arm free, then marched through the crowd to the exit. My self-restraint lasted all of five seconds before I was going after her, cutting through the crowd, my eye always trained on her.

I had already gone too far down this road, revisiting that night, remembering the way she tasted and sounded, and how easy it was to make her shake, moan, and scream.

I burst out into the night in time to watch her disappear into the back of a cab. She couldn't be bothered to wait for an Uber. Neither could I, for that matter. It was my plan to get good and wasted after a long week, so I hadn't bothered driving, and now I followed her like some obsessed psycho in the next cab that came along. Rather than do something dramatic like demand he followed her, I rattled off her building address then texted the guys in our group chat, saying I scored for the night to get them off the scent.

Noah had once lived in the apartment she now inhabited.

There was no hiding for me.

Along the way, my determination only grew.

Fuck this.

Even after I made her come until her voice broke, she would consider going out and letting some worthless nothing talk and flirt with her, thinking he could get in her panties? She would stoop that low after knowing what I could do to her body? It shouldn't make my bones rattle with rage, but there was something about Rose that did that to me.

It was clear I hadn't made a strong enough impression. I would have to rectify that.

I paid using the touchscreen before hurrying out of the car, crossing the sidewalk in a few long strides before pushing my way through a revolving door that opened onto a spacious, two-story lobby.

A lobby in which Rose stood, her back to the elevators, arms folded.

She was waiting for me.

She knew I was following her, and now I wondered who had the upper hand.

That question didn't stop me from following her into the first elevator to reach the lobby, neither of us saying a word. We didn't need to. We knew how this night was going to end.

10

ROSE

The doors were barely closed before he was on me.

My back hit the wall, and he held me in place, sandwiching me between his unforgiving chest and the cold metal. I felt nothing but heat.

The heat between us.

The heat from his breath.

The inferno erupting between my legs.

After two days of remembering and longing and even hating myself for letting him get to me, I needed this more than anything.

More.

Again.

Now.

"You think I would let some nameless, faceless nobody touch you?" One of his hands slid up my thigh, under my dress, until he cupped my ass and squeezed. I sucked in a gasp of mixed pain and pleasure. "You think he deserves to touch you? Taste you?"

I closed my eyes and stiffened when his fingers teased my inner thigh, then stroked my already throbbing lips through my panties. "You think he or your precious Landon or anybody else on this planet could make you come the way I did?"

I was tired of questions.

Tired of games.

Out of sheer desperation, I cupped the back of his head and sank my fingers into his hair, pulling him down so I could crush my lips against his.

By the time the doors opened, I was lost with no room for thinking. I could only feel, and it felt damn good when he scooped me up, and I wrapped my legs around his waist. The delicious pressure from his rock-hard bulge against my aching seam left me moaning into his mouth as he stumbled out of the elevator and straight ahead to my front door. I broke the kiss only long enough to punch in my key code, then let him open the door so we could escape inside.

Now, it was only us. No prying eyes, no questions, no reminders of our outside lives. There was nothing but breathless, dizzy desperation.

I kicked off my shoes while still in his arms, leaving them where they fell as he carried me across my apartment and into my bedroom. I hit the bed, but that was nothing compared to how hard Colton landed on me. I welcomed his weight, pressing me into the mattress because it was him.

All of him focused on all of me.

His teeth scraped the delicate skin of my throat before he moved lower, growling and grunting, while his tongue ran over my chest and dipped into my cleavage. "Oh God..." I sighed, arching my back to offer him more.

"That's right. Keep calling me that." His gaze flicked up to me, pinning me with a stare before he yanked down the front of my dress to expose my breasts. Taking one in his hand, he pulled my nipple between his lips and worked it into a tight peek, his tongue flicking the tip while I watched. It was so hot watching and feeling him.

"Fucking perfection, Rose." He moved to my other nipple, giving it the same treatment before adding, "I'm going to spend all night worshiping this body, make you come in every way possible. You'll be lucky if you're able to walk in the morning."

I answered the only way I knew how, by twisting his hair in my fingers and pulling his head down until he went back to work.

He slid an arm behind me and unzipped my dress. I lifted my hips, shimmying my way out of the black silk before he discarded it. It wasn't my style, something Sienna had talked me into, and I was glad she did.

His eyes had damn near popped out of his head when he first saw me in it.

Now, it was who knows where and soon followed by my panties. "Fuck me..." Colton groaned, getting up on his knees and looking down at my body. Without looking away, he reached down to his bulge, stroking it through his pants.

God help me...

I spread my legs and watched his gaze land between them. He swallowed hard while working his buckle, then unzipped his fly.

"Not yet," I whispered. "I want to see you. Take off your shirt." Because if I was going to lie here, naked and exposed, he was going to have to strip down too. I wanted the full experience. I wasn't going to leave anything on the table tonight since this would never happen again.

I couldn't let it.

I welcomed the almost painful throbbing of my clit as I watched Colton quickly unbutton and slide off his black button-down. His body was a work of art, a masterpiece, all chiseled muscle and smooth, tanned skin. Now I understood what he meant because I wanted to take hours to memorize every ripple, every ridge. To worship him.

It was when he left the bed to stand and strip off the rest that the already painful ache in my core threatened to kill me. He wasn't just gorgeous, charming, and wicked enough to make a nun rethink her vows. He was hung like a horse. Big enough that a flash of doubt cut through me like lightning.

Could I handle that?

Would I be the world's biggest idiot if I didn't try?

He fished a condom from his wallet, which he tossed onto the nightstand before using his teeth to open the foil packet. I was transfixed by the sight of him unrolling the latex down his shaft. "Are you nice and wet for me?" he asked, staring down at my pussy again.

I reached down and dragged a finger between my lips, shivering at the way he groaned. "You tell me." I held up my finger, and he took it in his mouth, scraping his teeth over it before running his tongue along its length and letting out a throaty moan. I dropped back against the soft sheets and held my breath while he positioned himself between my legs, spreading them wider to make room before dragging his head through my wetness. That alone was enough to send shock waves of pleasure rolling through me.

"Fuck me," I begged.

Who was I? I didn't recognize myself, and I didn't care. None of that mattered when I had him, finally fulfilling fantasies I used to think I had let go of all that time ago.

All at once, a sharp, painful sensation tore through my consciousness as he began pushing his way inside me slowly, letting me adjust, filling me until I dangled between pain and pleasure.

Only one word would sum up everything I needed at that moment with my legs hooked around his hips, my arms draped over his shoulders, him fully inside me, our bodies joined, and his face hovering inches from mine. "More."

A ghost of a smile flashed across his face before he pulled back and filled me again. It felt better that time and even better on the next stroke. It wasn't long before I gripped him tighter, pushing against his ass with my heels, driving him even deeper.

This was what I was missing—total abandon and letting go of everything else. There was nothing but this, him and me in my bed. He was unlocking parts of me I never knew existed.

"You like this cock?" he grunted out through gritted teeth. He was losing his breath, and so was I. We both moved faster, using each other, letting ourselves be used.

I moaned, savoring the sensation of him moving inside me. The delicious friction, paired with his deep grunts, drove me closer. "Fuck me harder, Colton."

It was happening. I felt myself tightening, clenching around him. The tension was too much. I was almost afraid.

There was no fighting it, though. "I'm coming!" I whined, dragging my nails across his shoulders and bracing myself.

"That's right, baby." His breath was hot against my ear, making me whine again. "Come on my cock. Come for me, Rose."

That was it. Those four words. They sent me flying over the edge into sweet darkness, where there was nothing but the satisfaction of Colton groaning against my neck as he came, losing himself in me the way I lost myself in him.

What a shame that blissful haze didn't last forever. Almost as soon as the wave subsided, regret started filling in the empty space.

He rolled away from me with a sigh, flopping back with his head against a pillow. Without saying a word, I got out of bed, wincing at the soreness that came with every step. I thought I heard him chuckle, the arrogant prick, but ignored it on my way to the bathroom to clean up.

Now I knew what it meant to be thoroughly destroyed by Colton Black. How was I supposed to go back to sleeping with normal, ordinary men after him?

What was I thinking?

I splashed cold water on my flushed face, so cold it stung.

He was one man.

One ridiculously hot man.

Ridiculously well-hung.

Ridiculously, insanely good in bed.

But he was not the end-all, be-all. No matter how much my still-quivering pussy wanted to believe otherwise.

I left the bathroom with renewed confidence, reminding myself what this was all about. He was reclined with his hands folded behind his head, making his biceps bulge, while a sheet barely covered him from the hips down. He was living, breathing sex, and he stared at me like I was a feast he couldn't wait to enjoy.

"I think we need to get a few things straight," I announced before either of us could do anything stupid, coming to a stop next to the bed.

One of us needed to be the mature one here.

He pursed his lips, lifted his brows, and sent fresh hunger slithering through me like a snake. I had to get a grip on myself before I forgot what I started talking about in the first place. "Well? Illuminate me, boss," he teased in a low voice that damn near made my toes curl.

I had to ignore the smart-ass remark. "Nobody can ever know about this. For many reasons. Our families, your sister, my brother. It would be…"

"A fucking headache," he concluded, nodding. "Agreed."

"When we're at work, we keep it professional."

He nodded again. "No arguments there."

"We're just having a good time, right?" I was starting to lose my nerve. Maybe because I really and truly heard myself. I was making excuses, rationalizing, but the alternative was never having him inside me again, and I couldn't handle that idea.

He lifted his shoulders. "You know me. I'm all about having a good time. I don't do relationships, remember? And you still have your sights set on a third-rate version of me, so we both have plenty of reasons to keep it casual."

"That's right." Was it wrong, though, to sort of wish he would put up an argument? He didn't have to be so quick to agree.

His dick was twitching beneath the sheet by the time he sighed. "Well? I'm pretty sure I said something about all night long. Do you think you can handle me?"

I honestly didn't know, but I was willing to find out.

Nothing and no one could've stopped me from trying.

11

COLTON

"Looking good."

Last week was the first week of renovations for the store. Sure, it had potential, but part of me wondered whether we could pull off such a complete transformation in a handful of weeks.

There was still a long way to go, but as I examined the work done to wall off the back third of the space to create offices, I couldn't ignore a feeling of pride. No, I hadn't framed the walls or put them up, but I'd watched it happen. The skill and speed with which the crew worked left me with a grudging admiration for whoever did the hiring around the company. I knew it wasn't my father since he didn't bother with shit like that. It was beneath him.

"The day's early too." Rich, the foreman, looked up from the blueprints spread out over a worktable. "You think the boss will be happy with it?"

Rose's timing was impeccable. "No wonder my ears were burning." She stepped through what would be a doorway, but at the moment, it was a hole in the wall. Her brilliant smile spoke volumes. "This is great. I can't wait for the furniture to get in."

"We still have time before that happens." Rolling up the plans, I grunted in acknowledgment of Rich announcing he was going to grab a coffee from the café across the street.

Once he was gone and we were somewhat alone, I shot a pointed look at the table where Rose had laid back to let me eat her out. That was almost a week ago, and since then, I was much more familiar with her body. What she liked, what made her scream, everything in between. "We'll have to christen this place once everything is finished," I suggested in a low voice meant only for her.

Her lips pulled into a thin line. "What did we agree on?" Fuck, if she only knew what it did to me when she got all hard-ass and tough. I was more determined than ever to have her here in every conceivable way.

"Keep it professional?" Looking her up and down, I added, "Though you're not playing fair, looking the way you do today."

She looked down at her sleek pantsuit. "This? Even this turns you on?" she asked in disbelief.

"When those pants look like they were sewed on?" I growled at the sight of her firm, peachy ass. "Remind me to take a bite out of you later."

Understanding flickered in those emerald depths, but there was something else in them. Hesitation. Regret?

She didn't keep me waiting for clarification. "He's coming by to check out the space, and we're going for coffee."

So much for foreplay. My mood dropped when I realized she wore the suit for Landon. "Then, by all means, let's fuck around," I suggested. "If he comes in and catches me feeling you up, he'll ask you to move in with him by the end of the day."

"Let's not and say we did." She folded her arms, popping one hip out to the side, and the defiance in her smirk was too much. I had to wipe that look off her face and replace it with open-mouthed ecstasy.

"Hell, he might even learn something," I pointed out, almost salivating at the memory of making her beg for more until we passed out around dawn on Saturday morning. I'd lost track of her orgasms along the way. "You'll end up thanking me later," I added with that in mind.

He probably didn't know where the clit was, much less what to do with it.

"Hello? Anybody home?"

What a corny asshole. I didn't know what pissed me off worse—the sound of his voice echoing in the wide-open space or the way Rose changed her posture, standing straight and throwing her shoulders back before striding out to meet him in what would soon be the store's showroom. *I may as well not exist.*

"You've already come so far! This is incredible." When Landon looked over the top of Rose's head to find me approaching behind her, he leaned down to kiss her cheek, offering her a warm grin. "I might have to hire the company to do some renovations at my new house."

Christ, he was exhausting with that fake politician's smile.

"I can't say enough about the work the company has done for us so far." Rose's smile looked a little strained. Somebody had to tell her she didn't need to try so hard.

"Is that what brought you two together?" Landon asked. He was digging for information, but I wasn't fooled.

"Oh, no. I mean..." Rose sputtered, which gave me no

choice but to drape an arm around her waist and pull her close.

"What she means is we've already known each other for a long time, but coordinating this project brought us closer together." She stiffened when my hand grazed her ass but managed to giggle at my explanation.

"I didn't know you were involved in the family's construction business." Landon slid his hands into the pockets of his puffy vest, studying me. "Hell, you always talked about how you would rather do anything else than work for Barrett. What changed your mind?"

"I grew up." Narrowing my eyes, I added, "Just like you grew up and decided you wanted to get into politics. You always talked about living off the money your mother's family left her. Time changes things."

"We'd better get going." Rose's voice was much too bright and chipper. Looking up at me, she touched a hand to my chest. I could almost believe the adoration radiating from her when she purred, "Do you think you could spare me for a little bit?"

"I don't know." I tightened my grip on her, growling. "You know I hate being away from you."

"Hey, hey!" Landon held up his hands, laughing too loud. An empty, flat sound. "I'm not trying to get in the way of love."

"There's nothing wrong with having coffee with an old friend." She drove her elbow into my side until I released her. "Come on, Landon. I would love to hear more about your campaign plans." With one more look over her shoulder, Rose took Landon by the arm to lead him out.

There was nothing for me to do but watch them go while something hot and caustic boiled in my guts. Why did it have to be him? Why did it have to be her, for that matter? It was bad enough I could barely hear myself think over the whining of saws in the parking lot. It was like a sick contest to see what could give me a headache first—the noise or the idea of Rose moving on to Landon after being with me.

It didn't hit me until then that I expected her to forget about him after the night we'd spent in her bedroom.

That was fucking stupid.

At the same time, I sent her a text. I couldn't let it go and let her smile sappily at him without reminding her of what she was missing.

Me: *Remember to let him know you like your ass spanked when you're getting fucked from behind.*

I would've bet my Bugatti she would blush when she read it. I was grinning to myself, sitting down with my MacBook to fire off a status report on our progress, when my phone buzzed.

Rose: *Could you please have a little decorum, for God's sake? Now is not the time.*

Me: *But it's the time for you to try to get into his khakis? I thought this was a workday. Make up your mind.*

Rose: *I'm turning off the phone now.*

Me: *But your boyfriend misses you already...*

Rose: *Grow up.*

I tossed my phone onto the table with a growl and forced myself to work on the reports, though my thoughts were miles away. No, not that far. A few hundred feet, the distance from where I sat to the café.

Minutes passed.

This wasn't me checking the time and keeping tabs. What could they have to talk about for forty-five minutes? The crew went outside to eat lunch, leaving me alone in the building, and still she wasn't back. My hand moved toward my phone, prepared to shoot her another message, but good sense stopped me.

I didn't beg a woman.

That wasn't me.

Yet there was no keeping my heart from beating double time when her heels clicked against the hardwood floor. *What the hell is up with me?* I stood before she rounded the doorway and charged at me, slamming her purse onto the table, murder flashing in her eyes. "How immature can you be? There I am, trying to have a conversation, and all you can do is—"

Before she could say another word, I took her by the waist and yanked her close, covering her mouth with mine and silencing her tirade. Coffee and sugar lingered on her lips. I plunged my tongue into her mouth, reminding her what she'd miss once this was over.

She didn't bother trying to fight me.

I backed her against the wall, then lifted her left leg and draped it over my hip. Caressing her ass, I nipped her lower lip, rolling my hips and driving my dick against her pussy. She whimpered helplessly, and something roared in my head. Something triumphant. She was mine. She didn't know it yet, was all.

When she arched her back, I slid my hand up her side and cupped her tit. She thrust her hips, humping me, and for one crazy second, I considered seeing where this went. How far we could go. My cock was hard as steel and aching to sink inside her tight sheath.

It was the sound of footsteps as one of the guys came in from lunch that convinced me to stop. Not much else could have—maybe the entire building falling on our heads. I let her up for air but kept her pinned where she was and watched as she blinked away the haze I'd wrapped her in.

"Tonight," I growled out. "I expect you at my house by eight o'clock sharp."

The narrowing of her eyes was a challenge. She thought she could fight me. "What if I don't care what you expect?"

"We both know that's a lie." Running a hand down her side, I took hold of her hip and pulled her flush against my erection again. "Don't allow me to show you what happens when I don't get what I want when this is so much better."

I knew before I let her go, she would be there. I could practically feel her resistance melt under the heat of my touch before taking mercy and backing away.

"You might not want to hold your breath," she insisted, straightening her clothes and running a hand over her hair to smooth it down. "I don't like being told what to do."

"You don't seem to mind when I tell you to come for me."

As I walked away, she gritted out, "Asshole."

I laughed over my shoulder. "Tell me something I don't know, boss."

12

ROSE

This was what my life had come to. Obeying Colton's wishes, driving down to his family's house because he told me to.

He would hunt me down at my parents' house if I didn't. I knew he would. That was all I needed, having somebody tip my parents off to a surly intruder on the security feed.

It was safer for me to do what he said.

Right. Keep telling yourself that.

Why did this have to be so damn difficult? Why couldn't I have fun for once without feeling like I was walking a tightrope? A single wrong move, and I would end up falling without a net to catch me.

I gritted my teeth with determination as the Black house loomed ahead. It was close to the beach, almost cozy despite its sprawling size and grandeur. I had always felt at home there, but a lot of that could be chalked up to how close we'd always been with the family.

I didn't want to imagine what they would think about me showing up for what was essentially a booty call. The memory of Mom's reaction when she thought I was interested in Colton added to the conflict churning in me as I pulled the Mustang to a stop beside his Bugatti. It was a few minutes to eight on a beautiful, clear night.

And I was about to debase myself again, jumping when Colton snapped his fingers.

I had to end it. Tonight. We couldn't keep doing this. I had to get out while I still a scrap of self-respect left.

Colton opened the door at my knock, and all my determination melted under the heat of his stare. Somehow, he managed to make a plain, white button-down shirt look painfully sexy. The hint of a broad, tanned chest, thanks to a couple of opened buttons, made me lose my breath.

His knowing smirk didn't help. "Right on time. The food is still hot."

"Food?" I caught the faint aroma of garlic in the air as I stepped into the familiar entry hall. He didn't waste time on formalities, heading straight for the kitchen and leaving me with nothing to do but follow.

I wasn't used to the house when it was otherwise empty and quiet, and the absence of light and laughter made me a little sad. He was here all alone, even if it was more convenient, as it was for me to stay at my parents' estate. It could get a little lonely in a big house.

"Have a seat. Wine?" He pulled a bottle from the wine refrigerator built into the kitchen's central island.

"Please." On the island sat a row of foil pans containing chicken cutlets, pasta, and salad. The paper bag bearing the name of one of my favorite local restaurants sat on the floor, telling me this would be a good meal. "This smells amazing."

"There's plenty of it, as you can see." His soft laughter took me by surprise. "I might've ordered too much, but I know how to work a microwave. At least I know what I'll be eating the rest of the week."

"Depending on how much I eat tonight, you might not have much left." The truth was, I had been too nervous to think about eating until now, wondering what tonight was supposed to be about, expecting him to maul me the second I stepped over the threshold.

Instead, he was strangely...

... normal.

What a shame it made me slightly suspicious.

Get over yourself.

All right, so maybe I was secretly hoping he would maul me.

We dished up food for ourselves and took it over to the round table in front of a wall of windows overlooking the beach. Moonlight danced on the water, and a handful of glowing yachts bobbed in the distance. That, plus the dim lighting in the kitchen and the crisp, cold wine, made everything feel sort of romantic.

Was that the idea tonight?

What would I do if it was?

"This is incredible." I barely swallowed a mouthful of the tender chicken before taking another bite. "They've always been my favorite restaurant, hands down."

"I know," he said, cutting into his cutlet. "Remember Noah's graduation dinner?"

I put down my utensils, staring at him in amazement. "And I asked if we could box up the leftovers from the table so I could take them home? I can't believe you remembered that!" Not my proudest moment, but that was one hell of a meal.

He lifted a shoulder while I laughed, embarrassed. "Hey, I admired you for asking. I didn't have the balls."

"But you had the balls to go and volunteer when the hurricane hit?"

His gaze faltered, if only for a moment. "How did you know about that?"

"My mother."

"It was nothing," he said, raking a hand through his dark hair. "I did what I could to help families who just had their entire lives literally ripped from underneath them."

"I tilted my head to the side, studying him. "Why do you do that?"

"Do what?"

"Minimize your actions? Surely, you know you would have been their lifeline. And going into what was practically a warzone of damage and uncertain times, where your safety wasn't guaranteed either?"

"It was nothing, really." A slow smile spread on his lips, disarming me.

Why did he have to be this way? Just when I was convinced he was the most selfish, self-absorbed man to ever breathe air, he remembered something from years ago and then played down his philanthropic endeavors.

"So..." He swirled the wine in his glass, looking at it rather than at me. "How'd it go today with the Plastic Prince?" I assumed his almost brittle smile was supposed to be a parody of Landon's.

"Do you sit around all day, coming up with nicknames for him?" I asked while my fingers tightened around my knife. He was treading on dangerous ground.

"I'm too busy making sure your renovation is finished ahead of schedule." Lifting his fork to his lips, he added, "Then again, I am capable of multitasking."

"Congratulations. Do we have to talk about this? We were having a nice time, then you had to go and bring

Landon into it." I wouldn't have minded if it hadn't been for his attitude.

"I would love not to bring him into it." He took a deep gulp from his glass before giving me a sullen look.

What did he mean by that?

"Here I am, thinking you're a smart girl with a good head on your shoulders, but you're still wasting time trying to catch him."

"That's my business." I wished my hackles didn't rise defensively. It was too easy for him to get under my skin. "You don't have to worry about it."

"Maybe it pisses me off to know you'd be wasting your time with him."

"This again?" I pushed my plate away, groaning more out of disappointment than frustration. That's what this was about. He was buttering me up, lowering my defenses before attacking. "I know what I want. Why is that not enough?"

"He's never going to care more about you than he does about his career, image, position, and reputation."

I barked out a laugh. "You're such an expert?"

"Let's be real." He groaned, rolling his eyes. "We grew up in the same world, around the same people, and we've watched the same pitiful charades being acted out by countless couples. My mom's parents are a great example. They never had a real marriage. It's always been an act."

"I thought you didn't care about things like that?"

"*You* care about things like that," he reminded me. "Why would you put effort into somebody who's never going to put the effort into you? I don't get it, Rose, especially when you deserve better."

He shrugged a shoulder, flipping a switch and returning to his insolent, spoiled-rich-boy persona before pouring himself more wine. "But what do I know? All I care about is the next fuck."

It was a relief when he went back to his food since I couldn't breathe while he was looking at me. Where did all of that come from? And was he right? No, he couldn't be. It was his stupid, egotistical resentment. Nothing more. "I don't want to argue about this," I told him after catching my breath. "We could bicker back at the store if we wanted to."

"Good point. There are much better things we could talk about... and do..." Sitting back in his chair, his eyes crawled over me again.

That, I recognized. I wished my traitorous body would stop reacting to him the way it did, but there was no helping it. I was Pavlov's dog, and he had trained me well.

I had to try to resist, at least. "So that's what this is really all about. You buy me dinner and think that means I go to bed with you?" I summed up with a sigh.

"We don't have to go to bed. We can do it right here in the kitchen." He spread his thick thighs, then patted them. "I'm ready when you are."

"I haven't finished my meal." All it took was a suggestive comment or two and the memory of how hard he made me come—how many times I had—and I was wet and ready. He didn't need to know that.

"So what? I'd rather eat you, anyway. And you always seem to enjoy it." He was loving this, pushing my buttons, making me blush, and enjoying my discomfort. Not that I was uncomfortable with him. It was more me and how I'd promised myself I would end this tonight. I'd spent half the day coming up with arguments against this, for God's sake.

Right now, though? It seemed a lot more important to call the gorgeous, arrogant prick's bluff.

His eyes widened a bit when I left my chair. I was

wearing a knee-length dress, and with that in mind, I passed him in favor of taking a folded dish towel from where it hung over the oven door handle. "What are you doing?" he asked, at a loss for once.

Rather than answer, I showed him by folding the towel and letting it fall to the floor between his feet, then dropping to my knees on it. I said nothing, holding his gaze, daring him to look away as I undid his belt, then unbuttoned his slacks. He was already hard by the time I dipped my hand into the opening at the front of his boxer briefs and withdrew his thick cock.

I forgot how big it was. It was one thing to remember something, but another to hold it in my hand and feel it surge and twitch.

"What are you going to do now?" His voice was a deep, seductive growl that took my pussy from wet to dripping. Who was I kidding, thinking I could resist the opportunity to do this?

I pushed the guilt aside, lowered my head, and took Colton between my lips. His sudden, sharp intake of breath was intoxicating. I wanted more. I wasn't the only one powerless in all of this. He was just as weak for me.

The idea made me bolder. I watched every twitch of his face as I ran my tongue along the ridge of his swollen head. "Fuck me..." He groaned, closing his eyes, his head falling back, and the most delicious thrill ran through me.

I was going to make him beg.

"What do you want me to do with this?" I ran my tongue from his base to the bundle of nerves under its head, drinking in the sound of his tight, labored breathing.

"Put it in your mouth," he groaned out, reaching to take the back of my head and guide me.

I pushed his hand away, making his eyes fly open in

surprise. Without another word, I did as I was asked, taking as much of him as I could into my mouth and using my hand to handle the rest.

I took a few experimental sucks before letting him fall from my lips, stroking him with my hand. "Like that?" I whispered, grinning at his miserable groan.

"Suck me." He grunted, lifting his hips, desperate for my mouth.

The sight and sound of his need, combined with the feeling of this being so incredibly wrong, made my panties moisten. On my knees, on the kitchen floor, the remains of our meal still sitting on the table while my head bobbed rhythmically up and down. It was downright sinful, and I couldn't get enough of his soft, slurping sounds mixed with his deep, throaty grunts.

"You're so good... so fucking good to my cock. Take it, baby," he whispered, his breath quickening.

I took him as deep as I could, barely able to keep from gagging before raising my head until his ridge rested against the inside of my lips. I sucked harder, flicking my tongue along the underside.

His eyes flew open wide while a strangled cry tore itself from him.

"Hang on." He let out a regretful little groan as he gently but firmly pulled me off him. "I don't know what else you were in the mood for, but this is going to end real fast if you keep doing that." He tipped his head to the side. "Though it's not like I couldn't get it up again."

"Maybe I don't feel like waiting." I stood and hiked my dress up over my hips, taking his hands and silently instructing him to remove my thong. He fished a condom out of his wallet and unrolled it over his twitching length, staring at my sex as he did.

He didn't have it all the way unrolled before I climbed onto his lap and straddled him with the balls of my feet on the floor. "We can always finish dinner later," I whispered, impaling myself on him.

Just one more time.

13

COLTON

What was happening?

It was bad enough I'd let her stay with me after dinner earlier in the week when we were exhausted after hours spent letting dinner get cold while we went crazy on each other.

That was a first, spending the entire night. As it turned out, I didn't hate it.

I didn't hate it now, either.

Saturday morning, we were in my bed. Waking up next to her didn't carry with it any of what I used to assume—discomfort, awkwardness. There was none of that. There was only lying together, her head on my shoulder, her arm draped over my stomach.

If anything, maybe she had taught me something about myself. I could handle what used to be unthinkable, like ending every day this past week with the same woman.

It was amazing we'd managed to make it to work on time, to say nothing of productivity. Somehow, pretending we were nothing more than colleagues in front of the crew added something to the experience. I would catch her eye sometimes and wonder what they would think if they only knew what she was like behind closed doors.

For me...

... only for me.

And for somebody else, if she had her way.

It was good she woke up when she did, or else I might have spiraled to a dark place where Landon loomed over everything. "Good morning." Her voice was thick with sleep while she fought to open her eyes. "Sorry if I drooled on you."

Not exactly the sexiest thing she could say, but it made me smile. "It's not like I haven't had your bodily fluids all over me."

Would Landon ever make her come as hard as she did for me? Would he put in the work like I did?

Get the fuck over it. I had to get a hold of myself.

She sat up, stretching, glowing in the morning light coming through the window beside her. "I'm starving. Do you have anything in the kitchen for breakfast?"

"I have a few things. I usually—"

"You usually get breakfast someplace," she remarked, cutting me off and hopping out of bed, giving me a look at her delectable ass before she picked up the dress shirt I discarded on the floor last night as we fell into bed. With her hair still mussed from sleep and my shirt wrapped around her body, she was lucky to make it out of the room without me throwing her to the floor and fucking her senseless.

"Can I help?" I asked once we reached the sunlight-flooded kitchen.

She eyed me warily, taking in my pajama pants. "Don't know if you should do any cooking shirtless. I wouldn't want you to get burned." Something told me she didn't trust me at the stove. Neither did I, so I let it go.

"What are you making?" I watched her pull flour and sugar canisters from the counter, and then reach into the refrigerator for eggs.

"I was thinking pancakes. Sound good?"

My stomach growled in response. "Only if you make a million. I worked up an appetite last night. But then, you would know." I couldn't resist the urge to wrap my arms around her from behind. There was something strangely erotic about smelling my cologne on her skin, the way the sunlight shone through the shirt and revealed her curvy silhouette.

"We do want you to keep up your strength, don't we?" She flashed a naughty grin over her shoulder, and it occurred to me that I never considered sending her home this morning. That was what I should've done. Instead, we were living out this domestic thing in the kitchen, and I didn't hate it. It felt strangely natural.

She put me to work finding a frying pan, which I fished out of the cabinet under the counter.

The front door opened and closed.

Rose barely covered her mouth in time to stifle a gasp. She turned to me, her eyes bulging over the top of her hand, while someone punched into the alarm code in the entry hall. I could only imagine one person walking in here unannounced on a Saturday morning. I doubted Sienna got up this early, and she'd be in Manhattan now, anyway. Mom would have called first because she had common sense.

My father, on the other hand?

"Outside." It was a fucking joke, but it had to be done, ushering her through the kitchen and opening the back door so she could scurry out onto the porch. It was a chilly morning, and she was dressed in nothing but my shirt, but I couldn't do anything about that. It was either let her shiver for a few minutes or face World War III if she were discovered.

"Colton?" The prick's voice rang out, echoing through the first floor. "Is that you I hear?"

The idea of him heading upstairs and finding Rose's clothes strewn around the front bedroom helped me find my voice. "In the kitchen," I called out. There were ingredients everywhere. He would never believe I was the one doing the cooking, especially not for only myself. I rolled my shoulders anyway, standing straight and tall to face him when he entered the room.

He was dressed like he was on his way to play golf, something he had taken up in the past few years because he was determined to become a stereotypical old man. He took in the entire room in a single glance, his gaze lingering on the counter. "What are you doing?" he asked, finally looking my way.

"What do you think? I'm rowing a boat. It just looks like I'm making breakfast."

He sighed. "It's a little too early for your sarcasm, Colton. I came out for golf with a couple of clients and thought I would stop in to see how you're doing."

Right. "Out of the goodness of your heart?"

His lips pulled together, disapproving as always. "Is there anything wrong with that?"

"Not wrong. Just unusual. What, is it not enough that I'm sending regular reports detailing every aspect of the job? You have to check up on me on the weekends too?" Folding my arms, I had the satisfaction of watching him scowl, irritated that I could see through him.

"What's this really all about?" I demanded, half my focus on Rose. I needed him out of here, now.

Arching an eyebrow, he murmured, "I wasn't aware I

needed permission to visit my own house."

"You're checking up on me," I countered. "Why don't we drop the act and admit that's what this is?"

Shrugging, he asked, "Can you blame me?"

"Considering I'm a grown fucking man? I think I can."

He eyed the counter again, and the snide expression he wore left me gritting my teeth. "Since when do you cook?"

"Since when do you care?" I snapped. "Maybe I'm turning over a new leaf."

"Maybe you have one of your whores here."

Do not let him do this. Grinding my teeth, I muttered, "Last I checked, whores don't usually include breakfast in their prices."

"Spoken like someone familiar with them."

There was a lump of burning coal eating its way through my chest. How did he do this? It didn't matter how calmly I approached the bastard or how determined I was to be the bigger person. He was hell-bent on proving what a useless fuckup I was.

"It's none of your business. End of story." I turned away, tidying the counter. "I have shit to do today. If you're finished checking up on me, you can go."

"I'm not finished, thank you." He looked around the room, then out toward the back porch, where, as far as I knew, Rose was still hiding. He thought he was slick as if he was going to catch me in a lie.

He was, too, if he decided to take a look out there.

"What is it you want to know?" I demanded, my voice loud enough to pull focus back to me. "As per my reports, we're ahead of schedule. The windows weren't supposed to be installed until Monday or Tuesday of next week, but they're in now, and they look stellar. I had the team move on to finishing the back office yesterday, and they were able to start framing the dressing rooms. Everything's moving smoothly." That was when it hit me when his scowl deepened at what should have been good news. How stupid could I be? "You want there to be a problem, don't you? You're looking for any reason you can find to prove I can't be trusted. Why would you put me on this job if that's how you feel?"

His face turned stony. "Don't tell me how I feel."

"You act like we just met yesterday." I had to laugh. I couldn't help it. "Sorry to disappoint you, *Dad,* but everything's going better than we hoped."

"And you decided to celebrate by bringing last night's distraction to my home?"

"The ball's on you…" I laughed again, bitterly this time. "It was fine for you to whore your way up and down Park Avenue, all because you built a business at the same time? Here I am, kicking ass when you expected the opposite, and I'm not allowed to unwind over the weekend? I always knew you were a fucking hypocrite, but this is low even for you."

"Let me remind you who you're speaking to. You don't have the first fucking idea what it's like to really have a shitty father. A shitty home life. You should be appreciative after everything I've given you."

"If groveling is what it takes, you can have it. I didn't ask for any of the shit you gave me. I didn't ask for your last name. And I'll be goddamned if I spend the rest of my life kissing your ass because I happen to be the sperm that reached the egg first!"

"How dare you!" He was on the verge of explosion while my blood raced and a hot, sick feeling spread through me. I wanted him to explode. I wanted an excuse to knock him on his ass once and for all. My fists curled at my sides in preparation.

He jabbed a finger against my chest before I shoved his hand away. "Once this project is through, you're out of here. The only reason I'm letting you stay here is to keep you in the area so I can at least tell myself you might show up every day. But it's over after that."

"Fine by me. I'll move out today if that's what you want."

"No," he said with a nasty laugh. "I'm not going to give you an excuse to fuck off and skip work. You're staying here until the store opens."

He scoffed once more before turning his back to me, shaking his head as he sauntered out of the room and down the hall. "Make sure your whore doesn't steal anything on the way out. Or else it's coming out of your trust."

I was still staring toward the hall when the back door opened. "He's gone," Rose whispered behind me. "I heard him drive away. I... Colton, I..."

It was enough to put up with his disdain, low opinion of me, and determination to make me feel like shit.

I could not bear her pity. That was too much.

"You know what?" Without looking her way, I began cleaning up the meal that never was. "I just remembered I have some things to do this morning. It would be better if you went home now."

"Are you sure? I don't have to—"

"I'm sure," I snapped, cutting her off, then slammed the refrigerator door shut after putting away the eggs. "We already had a close call. It's better this way."

All I had to do was convince myself of that as she tiptoed across the room before her feet flew up the stairs.

Hell, maybe he had come at the right time. My arrogant asshole of a father might have saved me from making the mistake of getting closer to a woman who would never be mine.

14

ROSE

"Lunch break's over. We want these dressing rooms finished by the end of the day." Colton's voice rang out loud, sharp, and very much unlike his attitude during the first two weeks of the project. He was everyone's buddy then, getting along great with the guys, sharing their jokes, and, to my surprise, being an excellent manager overall.

I knew when the change came about. It broke my heart a little.

I had never seen that side of Barrett before. I'd never heard him sound so hateful. The ugly things he'd practically screamed at Colton were still rattling around in my head by Monday afternoon. It was as if he hated his own son.

I'd always figured Barrett was hard on him the way Dad was on Noah sometimes, but remembering the insults he'd flung made me want nothing more than to wrap my arms around Colton and tell him it would be all right, that we would make this work together.

But when I made the mistake of trying, he pushed me away, reminding me of my place in things.

Now, he was marching around the store, barking orders, and generally acting like an asshole. That didn't make what I wanted to ask him any easier to get out. The clock was ticking, though. We were just short of two weeks away from the project's completion, and I needed to stop thinking about Colton and lock Landon down. One more interaction with him would do the trick. I was sure of it.

This was why I had texted him earlier in the morning after a meeting with Dad to ask if he wanted to get together for drinks later tonight. His immediate, enthusiastic response had left me floating on cloud nine until I arrived at the store to find Colton berating the electricians for—as he put it—dragging their feet.

"Can I speak to you?" Rather than wait for a response, I tucked my hand in Colton's elbow and pulled him into my office. It was coming along but wouldn't feel quite right until everything was finished and the last touches were in place. I couldn't wait to bring in plants and personal items.

"What is it?" he grumbled. "I still have calls to make to one of the suppliers. They shorted us on drywall." Maybe the growl in his voice that tinged his obnoxious behavior with a touch of sexiness. Or maybe I was that hard up for him. I had to get over it. I would need to get him out of my system sooner or later.

Landon was the guy for me.

Responsible

Charming

Driven.

Taking my life in my hands, I said, "I was going to ask if you wanted to go out for a drink tonight. I invited Landon."

He closed his eyes and released a long breath that told me this wouldn't end well. "Why do I have to hear his name every goddamn day?"

"You don't hear his name every day, and a simple no would suffice." However, it wasn't the answer I wanted to hear. "Remember, this was your idea. I could easily tell him we broke things off."

His jaw tightened. "No, it's too soon for that."

"Too soon for what?"

"For him to think I'm stepping aside so he can take my place." Scoffing, he shook his head. "Fuck that. What time?"

"Seven o'clock." Now, I wished I hadn't set it up at all. Not with him in this mood. How could I have known Mr. Hyde would show up today in Colton's place?

"I'll be there. Now, if you'll excuse me, some of us have shit to do that doesn't involve making dates." I was left sputtering in disbelief while he marched out of the room.

It wasn't long before I heard him on the phone with the drywall supplier, yelling for answers. The sudden change had to be because of Barrett. If only he would let me in so we could talk about it, but I knew him too well to hope for that. He would rather internalize it and take it out on everybody else. Especially me, since I'd overheard the whole ugly fight.

I still knew his heart better than anyone.

"Landon! I thought that was you!"

Colton didn't bother stifling a snide laugh when we were interrupted for a third time no more than ten minutes after Landon joined us at a pub in town. This time, it was a woman I vaguely recognized. Mom had redecorated her vacation home at some point. They were around the same age, though that didn't stop her from practically shoving her boobs in Landon's face as she bent down for an air-kiss.

While the two of them talked, Colton leaned over in the booth, his lips brushing my hair before he murmured, "I've seen basketballs less inflated than those tits. Look how he's staring at them."

"Shut up," I hissed, though he had a point. "And maybe slow it down," I added, eyeing the two empty glasses already in front of him.

The defiant jerk lifted his hand to signal a passing server. "I'll have another."

"None for me," I murmured when she looked my way. I was still nursing my first glass of wine. Landon, meanwhile, was too busy discussing the campaign with Basketball Tits.

"Could you at least behave yourself? Loosen up," I whispered to Colton.

Draping an arm across the top of the booth, he gave me a careless shrug. "I'm fine. I don't need to loosen up. You're the one who historically needs to loosen up, remember?"

"Colton, Rose, do you know Paula Davies?" Landon was definitely pouring on the charm tonight. "Her husband is one of my campaign's most generous donors as of this week."

"Well, there's no accounting for financial decisions." Colton pretended to laugh at what wasn't a joke while shaking Paula's bejeweled hand. "Don't listen to me. Landon and I go way back. It's what we do."

Landon didn't look like he saw anything funny about it. "The good old days. A lot of water under the bridge since then," he pointed out in a quiet voice.

"I won't keep you," Paula insisted. "Though I did want to invite you out to our yacht next weekend, Landon, for some fishing. Johnny has been dying to show off his new toys."

"I figured she was showing off his new toys right now," Colton muttered, barely trying to lower his voice as he eyed her very tight, low-cut sweater. I kicked his ankle under the table, but he gave no reaction.

"Sorry about that." Landon only had eyes for me once Paula left, and he sounded chagrined. "I can't go anywhere. So much for a private life."

"Isn't that the trade-off?" Colton accepted a fresh drink, lifting it like he was saluting Landon. "I'm not sure I could handle the scrutiny."

"But then, you have plenty worth scrutinizing," Landon countered, lowering his brow.

Shots fired. That was the first real, certifiable insult he had slung so far. I almost respected him for it.

Colton countered by drawing me closer, his lips grazing my temple. "This one made an honest man out of me," he replied. He may as well have peed on me to mark his territory. But we were supposed to make this look real, right? Or was he only doing it to get under Landon's skin?

"I imagine a woman like Rose could turn anybody around," Landon agreed. "She's a hell of a lot prettier than any of the girls you were involved with back in school too. And there were plenty of them, Rose, trust me," he added with a wink.

"Good to know you kept count," Colton gritted out, teeth clenched in what might have passed for a smile if we were strangers.

Landon was no stranger, which might have been why he doubled down, leaning toward me from across the table. "Just think... if you weren't with this slacker, you'd be with me on the campaign trail. We'd make the perfect couple."

Thank God my reflexes were quick when Colton practically launched himself from his seat, growling. "Who the fuck—" It was all he managed to get out before I took his arm in both hands and pulled down with all my might.

Thankfully, that was all it took to keep him from grabbing Landon and rearranging his face.

"He's only joking," I murmured as I cozied up to him, wearing a cheesy smile to hide my horror.

Landon shrugged with a sigh. "I guess it's a shame you got your hands on her before I did."

"I've always been good with my hands," Colton replied, this time kissing my cheek before nuzzling my neck until Landon scoffed softly and looked away.

This was a fucking disaster.

It was a relief when Landon caught sight of something behind me and waved. "Sorry to cut this short, kids, but I made a dinner reservation here with some potential donors after Rose invited me out."

Taking my hand, he lifted it to his lips. "A pleasure, Rose. We'll have to do this again real soon," he said, holding my gaze a long moment before nodding to Colton while making his escape and calling out to his guests.

"Dickhead." Colton sneered into his glass before draining what was left. "I hope you don't mind being second to his donors."

I was beginning to question that myself, but I sure as hell didn't need to hear it from him. "You're getting drunk. I'm going home."

What the hell had I been thinking, setting this up?

I wasted no time grabbing my purse and heading out the door without bothering to check whether Colton would handle the tab. He wasn't my problem, not him, his shitty attitude, or his casual cruelty. Why did he have to make me feel so low about something I wanted?

"Wait a second." I was halfway to my car when he caught up to me, grabbed my wrist, and turned me around. "Where are you going?"

"I told you. I'm going home. *Alone,*" I added.

"Says who?" The smell of scotch filled the air when his breath hit my face.

"Says me." I pulled my arm free, looking him up and down as if it was the first time. "You don't get an all-access pass to me whenever and wherever you want. Especially after you acted like a raging asshole in there and made a fool out of me... and yourself."

The way he flinched was gratifying. He needed to hear it and be insulted.

"Let me get this straight." With his hands on his hips, he stared down at me in something like disbelief. "I have to go to all this trouble in front of that dickhead, and I don't get anything out of it?"

Everything in me recoiled from his casual nastiness. "To think I felt sorry for you," I whispered, shaking.

"Sorry for me?" His eyes bulged before he let out a snide laugh. "Give me a break."

"I thought maybe you were misunderstood. But no, you're just a raging asshole who can't handle anybody else playing with your toys. Well, guess what?" I spat, relishing the surprise on his drunken face. "I'm not one of your toys. I am not yours. And the next time you want to piss all over something to mark your territory, choose somebody else. It won't be me."

He didn't bother stopping me when I turned away again, and by the time I was behind the wheel, he was already gone. Where? I had no idea.

Not that it was my problem in the first place.

Yet, why did it feel like it was?

15

COLTON

"We have a problem."

This was not exactly what I wanted to hear from Rich before I'd closed my car door or ever. I'd imagined Rose's return for the first time since the disaster with Landon would be the focus of my day.

Only, our foreman wouldn't look so grim over a fight I had with her three days ago, and he wouldn't greet me at my car rather than wait for me to get inside. This had to be important.

He cast a worried look toward the store, rubbing a hand over the back of his neck before grunting. "We got a call from the carpenter in Sag Harbor. Those shelving units that were supposed to come in today? He's saying they're going to take another week."

Immediately, my brain started clicking, running through the plans for the rest of the project. The shelving had to be installed before anything else was brought in. Displays and counters couldn't be put in place before the shelves were, as the men would need room for ladders and tools to mount them safely. In other words, it would push the entire project off a week which meant delaying the opening.

"She's losing her shit," he muttered, grimacing. "I was going to call the main office, to see what we can do to expedite things."

"No." I would not let him take this to my father. No fucking way. It wasn't my fault the shelving was late, but it was up to me to do something about it. "I'll handle it." He fell in step with me, entering the store, where Rose was in the middle of a rage.

When she noticed me enter, she practically flew across the room until she was almost in my face—flushed, breathing hard, her eyes dangerously bright. The crew hung around here and there, looking like they wished they were elsewhere.

"That's it," Rose declared. "We're fucked. We are absolutely fucked! There is no way we're getting this done on time if the shelving is a week late."

Reflex left me wanting to take her by the arms to touch and calm her, but I couldn't do that in front of an audience. "We'll figure it out."

"Like what? Those shelves take up one entire goddamn wall!" She swept an arm to the side, indicating the wall in question. "Everything else hinges on them being installed! The press releases went out ages ago, and I can't open a half-finished store! What are we supposed to do?"

When unshed tears sparkled in her eyes and her chin started to tremble, something in me snapped. I couldn't let this happen. "I'll take care of it," I told her.

"What are you going to do about it?" she asked, tears edging her voice. It would kill her to break down crying over this, especially with the crew around. Their embarrassment hung thick in the air.

"Hey, guys. How about you take fifteen?" I watched them practically flee the store. They were decent men, hard-working, and easy to get along with, though we had little in common. That didn't mean they felt comfortable watching a woman break down.

Once they were gone, I led Rose to her office and placed her in front of a chair. "Sit down, take a breath." When she didn't invite me to fuck myself for telling her what to do, I knew she was truly at the end of her rope. I kept that in mind as I pulled up the carpenter's contact in my phone.

It rang once before he answered. "Colton Black, good to hear from you. Listen, I told Rose earlier—"

"Hello to you, too," I barked over him. It was bad enough this guy was trying to fuck me after he'd worked with both of my parents for years. But steamrolling me before I could say a word? I wasn't putting up with that shit. "I understand the shelving you *guaranteed* to be delivered by this morning is now delayed a week. Explain to me how that happened."

"Well, you see—"

"Wait," I decided, cutting him off again. "I just remembered I'm not interested in your explanation because you've had weeks to finish this commission, and I find it hard to believe you didn't know until this morning that you were running behind. How does that happen? Can you tell me?"

"Hang on now."

"Here's what's going to happen." I glanced at Rose, who watched in wide-eyed silence. "You are going to have those shelves at this location by eight o'clock Monday morning, no excuses. Don't tell me you can't get it finished by then. Bring in help if you have to. Skip sleep, it doesn't matter. Otherwise, since you are officially in breach of contract, we'll take you to court. Can you afford that?"

Was it possible to hear somebody pissing their pants

over the phone? "What are you talking about? Breach of contract? That's ridiculous!"

"There is a stipulation that any change in delivery had to be announced at least seven business days before the agreed-upon date. Or did you not read what you signed?" I had the pleasure of watching Rose's eyes grow wider until they bulged from her head, but the weak sputtering on the other end of the call truly made this worthwhile.

"Okay. Wait a second."

"I don't have a second to waste," I told him. "Neither do you since you have shelving to complete in time to get it here by eight o'clock Monday. Do we understand each other? Or should we call the lawyers now rather than wait?"

After a silent beat, he grunted. "We'll pull overtime this weekend. I'll have it there."

"I knew we could come to an understanding." Ending the call without bothering to say another word, I placed the phone on the table and turned to Rose. "There you go. We're only losing a few hours in the grand scheme of things, and we're still running ahead. Everything's on track."

Her mouth moved silently before she croaked, "How? I... how?"

Laughing, I asked, "Any other fires you need me to put out today?"

I wasn't prepared for the way she launched herself into my arms, but I wasn't unhappy about it, either. How was I supposed to convince myself there was a way to get used to never touching her again? How, when it felt so damn right, holding her close, feeling her body against mine?

"Oh my God. Thank you. Thank you so much!" She pressed her face to my neck, and I closed my eyes, soaking her in.

"Shit, I helped you out while verbally assaulting somebody. It's practically my ideal day." I chuckled.

She pulled back, her cheeks damp with tears. "I never even thought to look at the contract. I was too busy freaking out. But you knew off the top of your head."

"I did my homework. It helps that there's a standard contract for all vendors and suppliers," I pointed out.

Who the hell had she turned me into?

Since when did I give anybody else credit for my victories?

Since when had a victory felt so damn good?

It was more than the pleasure of holding her, hearing her praise the shit out of me. I made something happen. I kept the project on track, and I'd saved her from having a nervous breakdown. There were worse ways to feel.

She released a strained whimper before taking my face between her hands and pulling me down for a deep, fierce kiss.

So this was all it took to get her to forgive me? My grip tightened as the hunger I'd been battling for three days was finally satisfied—the taste of her, the sound of her high-pitched sighs as I ran my hands over her back, her ass, kneading the flesh I'd fantasized about.

I was almost sure I would never be able to do this again. Like I fucked us up for good. I'd told myself that was how it would have to be, but it was nothing but a weak attempt at getting over her.

"I need you," I groaned out between kisses. "Fuck, I need you so bad."

"Let's get out of here," she rasped while my lips skimmed her throat. "We can always come back."

That settled it. If she was into the idea, I wasn't going to waste a minute. We were still breathless when I locked an arm around her waist, leading her out of the office. At this rate, it would be a miracle if I made it to the house before I had no choice but to attack her.

All it took was a single look at the visitor standing in the middle of the showroom to make me forget about that. A very shocked, very red-faced visitor.

"Noah!" Rose fell back a step, bringing me to a halt. "I completely forgot you were coming in today!"

"Obviously." He went from staring at her to glaring at me like a bull ready to charge. "Tell me this isn't what it looks like. Tell me you aren't fucking around with my sister."

16

ROSE

This couldn't have gone worse. I went from the highest high to the lowest low and was still falling as my brother glared hatefully at us.

His attention swung from Colton to me. "What are you doing? Have you lost your mind?" he demanded.

"What do you think we're doing?" Lame, but it was the first thing that came to mind. Why volunteer information?

"It's pretty obvious. Look at you two!" He waved a hand, and it was only then that Colton let go of me. My heart dropped. Why did he have to do that?

"Why don't we take this someplace else?" Colton looked over his shoulder toward the back door. The crew was still out there, taking their break. "This isn't a good location."

"Oh, like I'm supposed to give a shit? All of a sudden, you're, what? A gentleman?" Noah spat. "How could you fucking do this? I flat-out told you not to!"

"Wow, wait a minute," I warned. What was I thinking, trembling in front of my asshole brother? Not a bad brother, not a bad person, but an asshole just the same. "Where do you get off? You told him not to? Seriously, who do you think you are?"

He scoffed. "We can talk about it later. I'm dealing with—"

"Fuck that. Talk to me." I touched a hand to my chest, where my heart beat wildly. "A grown woman. You don't know what you walked in on. Colton saved the whole timeline of the project and kept us from disaster."

"And he was about to collect payment?" The curling of my brother's lip was ugly and nasty. "I thought you were better than that."

"Enough with the big brother bullshit." Colton was still trying to laugh it off, but that was all for show. I heard the change in his voice. How it tightened, how he fought for every word. "It's all pretty simple."

Noah's snide laugh made my skin crawl. "Yeah, obviously. You couldn't leave her alone, could you? You couldn't stand the temptation. She wants to be somebody, but you have to ruin that!"

"How would he ruin anything?" I was shouting, we all were, and by now, there was no way they couldn't hear us outside. My skin burned with humiliation, but I pushed through it. "You're underestimating me, and you're underestimating him!"

"This isn't about you," he snapped, pointing to Colton. "It's about him! He knew better! He just couldn't resist an easy fuck."

He may as well have hit me. The force of his ugly words knocked the air from my lungs. I never thought something like that would come from my brother's mouth.

I didn't know him.

It wasn't enough for Colton to stand by and take it. I watched in horror, frozen in shock, as he took two long strides toward Noah. When he cocked his fist back, I pulled in a breath, prepared to beg him not to do it. Anything but this.

It was too late. His fist shot forward, hard enough to make Noah's head snap to the side once he made contact.

"Stop!" I screamed, but it was no use. Noah recovered quickly, taking Colton by his collar. My stomach flipped at the sound of his fist hitting flesh, at Colton's groan, and at the sense of everything falling to pieces. It was all crumbling, turning into nothing. My family, my reputation. Everybody would know now.

"Would you please stop?" I was on the verge of tears, shaking, but neither of them heard me. How could they? All they could do was stare daggers at each other, their fists raised, ready for a full-on brawl.

I grabbed the closest thing I could get my hands on, a broom propped up against one wall. "I said stop!" I screamed, swinging the broom between them, holding it at chest height. It wouldn't do anything to stop them, but it was enough to startle them into taking a breath instead of making an unforgivable mistake. "For fuck's sake. This is not happening here, do you understand? This is my store! You are not tearing the place up like a couple of children!"

Colton touched a hand to the corner of his mouth, where a thin trickle of blood oozed. He studied his fingertips before lifting his eyes and looking at my brother. "Now I know what you think of me." His disappointment made my heart ache.

Noah shrugged. "What else am I supposed to think? You've pulled some shit, but this is the lowest." He was starting to get himself worked up again, breathing hard.

It hardened me and got my blood boiling. My hand closed around the broomstick tight enough to make my joints ache. "You hypocritical son of a bitch," I muttered. It was nice watching his face go slack, watching him fall back a couple of steps like he was genuinely shocked his little sister had something to say. "All of a sudden, you're my protective older brother? You've spent your entire life just as self-absorbed as you're accusing Colton of being now. It's all fun and games when the two of you are running around chasing pussy, then discarding it when you get bored, huh? Then you go and put me in the same category as your whores? How fucking dare you!"

"Don't say things like that," Noah warned. He even looked grossed out. My full-grown brother was scandalized because his sister used a dirty word. It was beyond pitiful.

And maybe it was because I saw how pathetic he was that I was able to keep going as I lowered the broom. "I'll say whatever I want. I don't need you to police my language or fight my battles. If you have a problem with your best friend being with your sister, so be it, but don't act like it's because you want to protect me. I don't need your protection. Got it?"

"He's only using you." He snarled at Colton, who scoffed and shook his head before turning away. "That's all this is. Are you going to spend another two weeks crying your eyes out over him when he breaks your heart this time?"

"What the fuck?" Colton cocked his head to the side as he turned around, looking at Noah before turning to me. "What does that mean?"

Ignoring him, I told Noah, "I am not a teenager anymore." Dammit, I was trembling harder than ever. If I wasn't a teenager, why was I reacting like one? "We're adults now. I won't have you barge in here and ruin my store all because you have to be the big, tough guy. It's time for you to leave."

He released a choked laugh, staring at me like he

expected me to change my mind. "You can't be serious. If you think I'm keeping your dirty little secret, think again."

Everything in me recoiled at the thought. Dad would know, Mom would know, Colton's parents. Oh God, what would Barrett say now? And Sienna! What would she think?

A sense of ease washed over me. Nobody could've been more surprised than I was when I felt it, especially in the heat of the moment. It left me calm, clear, and unflinching. "If you can't keep this between us, it only proves my point."

"What is that?" He sneered, folding his arms. The splash of red across his jaw was going to turn into a bruise, but he didn't seem to notice it.

I wished Colton had hit him harder.

I was the one who stopped it, though.

"You don't care about what's really best for me. If you did, you would know it's not a good idea to run around broadcasting this, especially at such an important time." I waited for this to sink in, and I watched as his expression softened a little. Enough to tell me he was listening. "If Colton has ever been a friend to you, you'll keep your mouth shut. And I know he has, no matter what you think right now."

"This isn't over," he promised with a growl that almost set my hair on end. He wanted to rip Colton's head off. That was obvious. "We're going to revisit this."

"I can't wait," Colton told him, firmly standing his ground. "Do you need help finding the door?"

"You fucking bastard." That was the last thing Noah spat before turning on his heel and storming out, slamming the front door. I stood there in silence, reeling long after the sound faded into silence.

"Fuck." Out of the corner of my eye, I saw Colton

touching his mouth again, wincing. "The timing couldn't have been more perfect."

Perfect wasn't the word I would use, but I understood what he meant. I was hollow inside, empty, shaking in the aftermath of so much adrenaline leaving my system.

"I need to get out of here," I whispered, almost surprised to hear myself say it out loud.

"That could be for the best," he agreed. Soon, his hand covered my shoulder, and his arms were open for me to step into the circle of his embrace. "I'm sorry for that."

Had I ever heard him use the word before? I couldn't remember. Miracles did happen sometimes.

"It's not your fault." I clung to him as tightly as I could. He had solved my emergency with the carpenter. If only he could have solved this too.

His chest rose and fell with a sigh. "I'm not sure what to have everybody do at this point. We were supposed to have the shelves in today. I could tell them to head out and get an early start on their weekend."

As much as I detested the idea, he made a good point. There was no sense in keeping them around with nothing to work on. It was a testament to Colton's management that so much had been wrapped up already.

Cupping my chin, he stroked my cheek with his thumb. The warmth radiating from his dark eyes melted me. "What do you say we get out of here after that? I can take you home."

"On one condition." I arched an eyebrow. "That it's your place we go to. Now."

If this was all going to end epically as soon as my family found out, I might at least get a little more enjoyment out of the arrangement where there was no chance of Noah walking in.

17

COLTON

We were barely inside the house before I was on her. Usually, I had a hard enough time keeping my hands off her, but something was different now. I knew why as I mauled her on the way across the entry hall, sliding my hands under her cashmere sweater until she moaned against my neck while we stumbled toward the sweeping staircase.

She had fought for me, defended me against her brother, and stood by my side. He'd slung the ugliest insults one friend could throw at another, and still, she was with me.

Rose landed on her ass midway up the stairs with me on top of her, leaning back so I could run my hands down her body. "Here. Right here." She slid her hands between us and worked my belt, then left it to me in favor of pulling her sweater over her head and unclasping her bra. "I need you. Now."

Not half as much as I needed her. My hands trembled with anticipation as I dropped my pants and boxer briefs to my knees. When I fumbled for my wallet, she stopped me. "I'm on the pill," she whispered, placing her feet on the floor and lifting her hips to lower her pants. "I want to feel you. I want you to come inside me."

Holy shit.

I wasn't about to say no to that. But when she went to settle her ass against the stair again, I shook my head and rolled her over. "Like this," I whispered, slapping her creamy ass before pressing my fingers against her firm flesh.

"Oh, yes," she breathed, arching her back and presenting herself to me. A prize—my prize—and her puffy lips glistened with excitement as I ran my head through her swollen folds. Her loud moans echoed through the wide-open space and turned into a high-pitched cry when I drove myself deep inside her tight sheath.

"My God!" she moaned out. There was nothing like the sound of her losing herself. She was completely free with no inhibitions, pushing back against my every stroke. I watched my glistening shaft disappear inside her. Christ, with no barrier between us, she was warm, tight, fucking heaven. "Harder, Colton, harder!"

Gritting my teeth, I took her by the hips, gripping her tight enough to make her gasp before rocking her forward again and again. My balls slapped against her clit, and her cries rose in pitch, her ass jiggling from the force of my thrusts.

"You like that?" My palm struck her ass, one side, then the other, until her white flesh turned red and her juices flowed.

"Y-yes!" she sobbed out in a stutter, losing herself. Her muscles began to tighten, trying to lock me in place, trying to milk me. And I loved it.

I loved all of it.

I wanted it forever.

"Fuck! Yes! I-I'm coming..." Her shrieks filled my ears, but it was the sensation of her pussy clenching around me that broke my control. I let go, let the rush overtake me, slamming home one more time before flooding her with my seed.

I was still emptying deep inside her as a single thought ran through my head.

We need to do this again.

She said nothing when I gathered her in my arms, still trembling after her orgasm, and carried her upstairs for more.

Deep down in what passed for my heart, I knew that tonight wouldn't be enough.

"My stomach is screaming for food."

"There's plenty down in the kitchen," I offered. Yet when she tried getting out of bed, I closed my arms around her, chuckling. "Go ahead," I teased. "Get up."

"Let go!" Her helpless giggles filled the bedroom as we tussled until she eventually gave up and draped herself over me once again. "Fine. But if I starve to death, it's on you."

I didn't want to let go because it would mean letting go of a moment I didn't want to end. Even so, my attention kept wandering back to the fight now that the blood had returned to my brain.

Noah's insults echoed in my memory until I couldn't take it. "Can I ask you something? About earlier."

She groaned and weakly slapped my chest. "Can we just forget it?"

We both knew better than that. "I'm curious about something he said. What did he mean, you cried your eyes out for two weeks because of me?"

She went stiff and looked away with a soft sigh. "He shouldn't have said that. It wasn't his place."

"That doesn't answer my question."

"It was about... Jesus, this is so pathetic." She insisted on avoiding eye contact, and her voice sounded small. Tight. "It was about... that kiss."

"What about it?"

Her mouth twisted into a smirk. "You remember it?"

"Sure. It was nice. I also remember wishing Mom hadn't found us out there."

"What happened after that? Once you left."

Strange. I could barely remember. "We went out, I think."

"Yes, you did," she confirmed in a flat voice.

It had to be something important, or she wouldn't have me on the spot like this. "I..."

"Let me help you. You stuck your tongue down some socialite's throat at one of the clubs you visited, you were caught on camera, and it was all over the place the next day. Hours after you gave me my first kiss. It was devastating," she concluded after rattling off the series of events like she'd been through them countless times.

Her first kiss.

And I had no idea.

"You should've told me."

She laughed softly. "Right. Because that would've been easy to admit. You had to know how much I liked you, though."

"I got the feeling you had a crush. And I sort of liked you, but I tried to brush it off. You were younger. I could talk to you, and that meant a lot." The memory made me smile fondly. Sitting with her in front of the bonfire. Talking on the balcony. The dozens of other times she'd been there to listen to what I didn't have the balls to say to anybody else.

"Noah's an asshole for throwing that in your face."

She wasn't wrong, but I couldn't completely agree. "He knows me too well, and that's my fault for being who I am. He's not wrong, either. You deserve better than me."

I hadn't planned on saying that. She had a way of unlocking me, forcing me to open up. It was nerve-wracking.

"He's still a prick," she insisted, sighing before lifting her head to give me a wry grin. "Excuse me. We can continue this when I get back." She wiggled her way out of my embrace and hurried into the bathroom. As I watched her bare ass retreat, it brought to mind a lot of things we could continue once she returned.

My head dropped to the pillow, and I stared at the ceiling. The light had changed, turning thin and weak, painting gray streaks overhead. We had spent most of the day in bed, and I wanted more.

Beyond tonight.

Tomorrow and the next day and next year.

It still wouldn't be enough.

It was sheer reflex, reaching for the phone when it buzzed with an incoming text. Not until I got hold of it did I realize it was Rose's cell buzzing, not mine. The new message was displayed on the screen—not Noah, as I would've expected, and not one of her parents.

Landon: *It was good seeing you the other night.*
Landon: *We should get together again. One-on-one this time.*
Landon: *Name the time and the place. I'm yours.*

My chest was tight enough to leave me struggling for air.

I sat up, replaced the phone, and stared at the closed bathroom door. She was humming in there, unaware of the fact that Landon was more or less hers for the taking.

I should have thanked him. He woke me up and brought me back to reality. This was never supposed to be forever. She would always want the kind of life he could give her. The run-in with Noah was a perfect example of how I would only hurt her. Who wouldn't be thrilled to know their sister, daughter, or friend was involved with somebody like him? Ari would never let the apple of his eye waste herself on a fuckup like me. Always looking for the next good time.

I'd be damned if I waited around for her to cut me loose. I didn't wait around for any woman to decide she was done with me, not even Rose Goldsmith.

It was time for me to remember who I was.

By the time the bathroom door opened, I was buttoning my shirt with my pants hanging open at my waist. She blurted out a laugh. "What are you doing?"

"Getting dressed. I've got things to do. It's Friday night, or it will be soon." Her mouth fell open, the only part of her that moved as she stood naked in the doorway while I finished buckling my belt.

I jerked my chin toward the nightstand, where her phone waited. "Landon is as good as yours."

"Wait. What?" That got her moving across the room, checking her phone.

"His texts came through while you were in the bathroom. Don't worry, I didn't open your app. But I saw them." Glancing her way, I added, "Congratulations. You got what you wanted."

Her face took on a sickly hue in the screen's glow. "Hang on."

"We had a good time. I delivered that, along with the

man of your dreams." Every word was sandpaper against my tongue, but I pushed through. "You're on your own from here."

"Oh. I see…" She sat on the bed, staring at the twilight beyond the window. "If that's what you want."

I paused in the middle of tucking my wallet into my back pocket, staring at her bare back. "Isn't it what you want?" I asked, aching to reach for her and touch her one more time.

Her head turned partway, giving me a view of her profile. *Say no. Please say no.* Her lashes fluttered, and she moistened her lips with her tongue while I hung helplessly, dangling on a string, waiting to find out whether I was good enough to wipe Landon Jones out of her mind.

"Sure." Her voice was flat, devoid of emotion. "I guess so."

I had to get out. I couldn't breathe. I couldn't look at her anymore. "I need to head back to my loft. Are you good showing yourself out?"

Her small voice barely reached my ears. "Did I do something wrong?"

"Not a thing. Like I said, we had a good time."

I know my place. I know I'm not wanted.

If only she would've stopped me. I had never wanted anything as much as I wanted her to tell me I was wrong, that she wanted me and for us to be together. This was who she had turned me into. A pussy who couldn't handle rejection and would've begged if I thought it would get me anywhere.

But then, she was the only person to stick up for me. She saw me and still wanted to know more. Rose made me feel like I was something better, more than most people had ever given me credit for.

I wasn't good enough for her, though. In the end, it was Landon she wanted. Leaving me to rush from the house, determined to get back to Manhattan and drink until I forgot Rose's name.

I had a lot of wasted time to make up for.

18

ROSE

Colton: *Checked in at the site. Shelves were delivered by seven forty-five. Crew is hard at work. I'll be working remotely since everything is on track.*

That was it. That was all he saw fit to send me first thing Monday morning after I had spent the weekend going over every detail of Friday, trying to figure out what was wrong, why he'd shut me out and walked away.

How could he have turned his back on me after everything we shared? It had seemed so real. After the fight with Noah, I thought I felt something real with him like we could be something more.

But then, what did he do? He threw Landon in my face and walked out the door.

In the end, it was best he stayed away. Our good time was over. Besides, that was all he was interested in, right? How had I lost sight of that? Because I chose to turn a blind eye to convenience. And it helped me get what I wanted, which was Colton's great, big dick.

If only it was that simple and all I needed.

"You know, the Davies' yacht was impressive." Landon was all warmth and cheer as he cut into a stack of pancakes.

Getting together for breakfast on Monday morning had been his idea, and I had accepted since it wouldn't conflict with the meeting I'd scheduled with Mom and Lourde regarding the design elements coming into the space this week. Now that the bones were in place, the finishing touches were all that was left.

As we sat in the café, the crew was across the street, making up for lost time with the shelves.

"Was it?" I asked. It wasn't easy to fake interest. I didn't care about their yacht, how great the fishing was, or the fact that the couple had invited Landon to come back whenever he wanted. The way he described the situation told me he was waiting for me to swoon.

"You should come with me next time." He waited a beat, then snapped his fingers. "What am I saying? I doubt your boyfriend would be a fan of that idea. Not that I blame him." There was a twinkle in his eye when he looked up at me from his banana nut pancakes.

"You wouldn't?" I asked, sipping my coffee.

"Hell, no. I wouldn't let you out of my sight, especially not around a guy like me," he added with a chuckle. "You might end up realizing what you're missing out on." Setting down his knife and fork, he turned his full attention to me. His gaze was heavy, serious. "But what do I know? Maybe you've already realized it. Maybe that's why you agreed right away to come out with me this morning."

It was almost funny. I honestly believed for the longest time that all of Colton's boasting was just that—prideful, ridiculous self-confidence, and outrageous ego.

Looking at Landon now, I couldn't remember why I wanted to be with him in the first place. A laugh worked its way out of me. Nobody could've been more surprised than I was to hear it. "What's so funny?" he asked, his smile slipping a fraction.

It took biting my tongue hard to put a lid on the laughter. "Nothing, really. Just one of those passing thoughts. Anyway, I appreciate the invitation, but I think I'll have to pass."

"What do you see in that guy? Straight up." His narrowed eyes darted over my face, searching for answers. "Why would somebody like you want to have anything to do with him?"

"It's not easy to put into words." I lifted my gaze to meet his, gritting my teeth against an angry outburst. *Where did he get off?* "And maybe none of your business, respectfully. I appreciate your concern if that's what it is, but there's no need for it."

He snickered and shrugged like he was disappointed but not surprised. "Some people just can't be told."

"I guess not." I'd had enough to eat. Besides, the company was making my stomach a little sour. I was so wrong about him. How could I have ignored what a self-absorbed, boring person he was?

Colton was right. I would never be more important to Landon than his image. He was only interested because he wanted to take me from Colton. I deserved better than that—someone who actually wanted me.

What a shame I couldn't find anybody who fit the bill.

"I have to go meet with my mom and her business partner at the store. But it was so good to spend a little time with you. Keep me posted on the campaign, please." I managed to sound genuine, or at least I tried. Colton would laugh himself sick if he knew.

Except he wouldn't because he would not speak to me.

I crossed the street on trembling legs once I recognized Mom's black Mercedes parked near the store. If Noah had spread the news about Colton and me, I would've known about it by then. No way my mother could have kept it to herself just so she could tear me a new one this morning. I needed to believe that as I entered the store, where the last of the shelves were being mounted.

Rich was talking with Mom when I entered. "I was just telling Mrs. Goldsmith here that we came in early to make sure the shelving was installed on time," he explained. "What do you think?"

What did I think? I was overwhelmed. More than anything, my heart ached. It should've swelled with pride, but instead, there was a stinging sensation behind my eyes. "It's amazing. I owe you so much for fast-tracking this."

"That's our job," he reminded me, waving a hand with a good-natured laugh. "After this, it's only a matter of installing the rest of the features."

"And then we get to pull it all together." Mom's eyes danced while Lourde entered through the back door, carrying a stack of folded drapes.

"A little help?" she called out, laughing. I could barely see her face, thanks to the fabric stacked in her outstretched arms.

"This is gorgeous," I sighed, touching the heavy silk. It would look stunning in front of the windows.

A handful of assistants scurried around as well, surveying the space and getting familiar with the placement of furniture—sofas, chairs, and footstools. Whatever it took to make the customers comfortable.

"I have to hand it to you." Lourde was gentle as she laid the drapes across a long table that had been covered with sawdust only a few days ago. "You pulled it together fast. It's like a miracle."

"Here we were, thinking we would have to cram decorating in at the last second." Mom threw an arm around my shoulders and squeezed me while Lourde beamed with pride. "I am over the moon for you, sweetie. This is a triumph. Your first big professional triumph."

"It's not only mine," I reminded her, fighting back a wave of emotion as Colton's image filled my head and made my heart swell painfully. "I couldn't have done it without Colton."

She winced. "He didn't make it too difficult on you, did he?"

"The opposite." I shot Mom a quick look at the mention of his name, but her expression gave nothing away. She was clueless. Thank God. "We would've been completely screwed without him."

"How so?" Lourde asked.

Interesting. After hearing Barrett hammering Colton, giving him hell, grinding him down, it was refreshing and reassuring to see nothing but adoration on Lourde's face. He deserved one loving parent, at least.

I gave them the CliffsNotes' version of what went down with the carpenter, leaving them wide-eyed and a little breathless. "But on top of that, he got along so well with the crew. He made them want to work hard, and he worked hard along with them. He filled in where necessary. He motivated them. He kept them on track, and we're ahead of schedule thanks to him. I can't imagine doing it without him, really."

Lourde clasped her hands together, glowing with pride. "I can't tell you how happy I am to hear that. I knew he would come through."

"Between you and me?" I added with my heart in my

throat. He probably wouldn't like it if he found out I said this, but I couldn't hold it in. "He would be a tremendous asset to the company if he decided to go full-time. He has that special touch. He knows how to get results."

Does he ever!

Heat bloomed in my core, but then that wasn't the sort of touch we were talking about. He had ruined me for all other men, plain and simple.

Thankfully, our discussions turned to decorating, and we confirmed when my office furniture would arrive. In other words, work stuff and putting the final touches on the finished product.

All the while, my mind was on Colton. I had spent months focused on this project, envisioning the day when everything was close to being wrapped up. I had imagined pride, excitement, and relief. I sure as hell hadn't imagined it feeling this flat. Anticlimactic. But he wasn't with me, so I couldn't share it with him.

If he didn't want me, I could learn to live with that. I had before. It would be easier if I knew he was happy. It was the best I could hope for now that he had walked away.

19

COLTON

The calendar alert had come through late last night. I had been summoned to Dad's office. No explanation, no option to reschedule. I was almost sure the prick had sent it so late because he'd been hoping I was partying and would show up hungover—another opportunity to make me look like shit.

A knowing grin tugged at my lips as the elevator car carried me to the top floor. He'd be disappointed to find me clear-eyed and sober. After a weekend-long binge, which had accomplished nothing but leaving me with a hangover, I was walking the straight and narrow.

The need to avoid my best friend played a part. Manhattan was a big place, but it had a way of feeling small at the worst possible time.

The elevator doors opened, and I stepped out, nodding at the receptionist as I passed. There was no need to escort me. I knew where my father's office was.

This was it—the one salvageable part of the past few weeks. I had crushed the job he gave me and was ready to tell him to shove it up his ass. I didn't do this for him. I did it for me.

And for Rose.

He didn't need to know that. I would keep it to myself to my dying breath. Nobody would know how I had embarrassed myself by falling for her when it was the last thing I meant to do.

It was a good thing all my father cared about was business. We wouldn't waste time on personal shit. We never did.

"He's waiting for you." His assistant popped up out of her chair and hauled ass to his office door, touching her knuckles to the wood before opening it. "Mr. Black, Colton is here."

I stepped into the room while she closed the door behind me, adjusting my cuffs before straightening my tie. "Good morning," I murmured to the man sitting at the big desk.

"I'm surprised to see you." Because why would he waste time on greetings?

"I had a feeling you would be." I sat without bothering to wait for an invitation, opening my suit jacket and crossing my ankle over my knee. "Now that you have me here, what do you want?"

"I would ask where this hostility stems from, but I don't have the time." He slid a folder across his desk, which I stared at rather than pick up. "This is an offer."

"For what?"

"Open it and find out."

Rather than drag things out any further, I did just that, flipping the folder open to reveal what looked like a contract. I flipped from one page to the next, stunned at the generous terms he'd outlined. I hadn't expected this. "I don't get it," I admitted.

"I know you would rather swallow nails than work here, but judging what you managed to make happen for the Goldsmiths, you'll sell yourself short if you don't pursue a project management position with the company. From what I hear, you're a natural."

"From what you hear? What does that mean?" Was I in some surreal dream? This wasn't my old man at all. Respectful, generous, praising me. "Are you sick? Is there something you're not telling me?"

His face went hard. "I'm attempting to extend an olive branch, and you make a joke."

"I wasn't joking. A few weeks ago, I was the scum of the Earth, accused of bringing whores into your home. Now, you want me as a project manager?"

He drew and released a slow breath, tenting his fingers beneath his chin. His face settled into a stern expression I knew too well. "All right," he eventually grunted out. "I deserve that. I'm sure my change of heart seems sudden. But results speak for themselves. The store has gone off without a hitch. Rose and Ari are thrilled, and when your mother told me what Rose had to say about your performance?" He shrugged. "It seemed like a no-brainer, bringing you in for good."

I hoped this would happen, didn't I? Until the moment I entered the room, in fact. I was sure he would offer to bring me on, and I couldn't wait to shove the offer in his face. Even now, with the folder in my lap, it occurred to me I could throw it across the desk and leave without another word. Let him know how much I gave a fuck about his job offer.

What I hadn't expected him to mention was her. "What did Rose tell Mom?" My fingers tapped the pages in my lap.

I was nervous. Me, Colton Black. Days spent telling myself I'd done the right thing by leaving had done nothing to scrub her from my soul.

He tipped his head to the side, studying me in a way that made me intensely uncomfortable. "She said you were a lifesaver. You were an excellent manager, the crew loved you, and you kept them motivated and on track. The store is set to open on time, and the client is beyond satisfied."

"She's happy. Everything's exactly the way it needs to be." It would have to be enough, wouldn't it?

Slowly, he tipped his chair back, his eyes narrowing. "Why didn't you tell me it was her?"

All the air left the room. "Pardon?" I choked out.

His face softened like he understood everything. "At the house. Colton, why didn't you tell me it was Rose?"

My insides turned to ice. This would blow back on her. She didn't deserve it. "Who said it was Rose?"

"Nobody had to," he retorted with a smirk. "You remind me a lot of myself right now. The way I was when I first fell for your mother. Suddenly, I cared about more than myself. More than my friends, having a good time. More than the business. Out of nowhere, my priorities realigned."

Before I could find the words to tell him how wrong he was, he stood, turning to look out the window behind the desk. "The truth is, you remind me a lot of myself. That's why I'm so hard on you. I know I am, but it's only because I've been able to see your potential all these years. Watching you waste it, squandering your time, treating life like an endless party that will never satisfy you come morning." Looking back at me, he concluded, "There's nothing that pisses me off worse than watching someone blow their potential. And you have it. It was never about the family's reputation or the company's image. I don't want you to waste your life. Take the offer, leave it, it doesn't matter. So long as you eventually do something that matters."

I couldn't remember the last time he spoke to me like that—calmly, honestly, and without the customary sarcasm and bitterness. "I'm not sure what that is yet." It wasn't easy to admit, especially not to him.

"Tell me you'll think about it, at least."

"I can do that." We were navigating uncharted territory. Slowly moving around each other, wary, but it was better than being at each other's throats.

He checked his watch, frowning. "I have another meeting in fifteen minutes. Are we all right here?"

"Sure. We're all right." It was foreign and uncomfortable, but I accepted the hand he extended and returned his firm handshake. He always found a way to throw me off balance.

Before I made my escape with the folder tucked under my arm, he called out behind me. "What about Rose?"

I opened the door, firm with resolve. "It was never going anywhere." Better to get used to the idea, repeating it to myself until the message sank in.

Noah was looking for Lucian when he stepped into the bar around the corner from his office. I appreciated my cousin's willingness to go along with a plan without asking questions.

He'd texted Noah to invite him for a drink at my request since I knew he'd never show if I asked.

It wasn't until he was halfway across the room, scanning the handful of tables currently in use, did Noah come to a stop, recognizing me waiting for him. There were already two drinks on the table, and I lifted mine in a silent salute.

"I should've known." With a disgusted huff, he turned, ready to leave.

"Are you that much of a pussy?" I challenged, smiling to myself when he stopped. "You can't face me? What happened to your balls?"

His fists clenched at his sides. "I have nothing to say to you."

"Then don't say a word. Let me do the talking while you sit and have a drink on me. *Sit,*" I snapped when he wouldn't move.

"I don't care about anything you have to say." Still, he dropped into the chair across from mine and picked up the whiskey waiting for him. Slouching, he rested the glass on his knee, staring at it rather than at me.

"Listen." I swirled my scotch, fighting to find the words. I had rehearsed this somewhat, but as usual, reality was a different matter. "It was only supposed to be fun at first. We were pretending to date so that asshole Jones would notice her."

"What did I tell you?" He guffawed, shaking his head. "I knew she would do something to get to him. I didn't know you would keep it from me."

"It wasn't your business. If Rose wanted you to know, she would've shared. I'm sure there's plenty she doesn't tell you and twice as much you don't tell her," I added because I knew him too well.

"Fake dating and fucking are two different things," he growled out.

I winced at his choice of words, then quickly recovered when he side-eyed me curiously. "And that's our business," I reminded him. "Not yours. I'm not going to apologize, and I'm not going to ask for forgiveness because I don't need it."

"Why did you arrange this, then?"

"I wanted to tell you it's over between us. You have nothing to worry about anymore." Throwing back what was left in my glass, I savored the burning sensation in my chest before grunting out, "They're probably planning their engagement party as we speak."

His stare was heavy. Intense. "Do you care about her? Tell me. It doesn't have to go any further than this room." His tone gave nothing away to explain the shift.

It shouldn't have been so tough admitting this to my best friend. We knew virtually everything about each other, but we had never ventured into this territory. It meant swallowing my pride, but I managed to admit, "I think I love her. But, like I said, it doesn't matter. She has what she wants."

He kept me hanging a few long, silent moments, waiting for his reaction. He didn't burst out laughing or throw the glass at my head. So, I chose to take that as a good sign.

"I wasn't going to tell you this. I mean, what did it matter?" He set down his whiskey before letting out a sigh. "I had dinner with Mom last night. She told me Rose gave up on Landon. She changed her mind."

Damn my heart.

Damn, the way it jumped in my chest, the way it took off like a racing engine.

She gave up on him.

She didn't want him.

Because I was right.

He was wrong for her.

After taking a deep breath, I forced myself to look at the truth rather than indulge in childish fantasies. "Good for her. I knew she would see the light. That doesn't mean she wants me, does it?"

He arched an eyebrow. I could almost see the wheels turning before he asked, "You mean it? You love her. Don't bullshit me, Colton. My sister is everything to me, and you, you've plowed through most of Manhattan."

He was right. But that didn't change a damn thing. "I do." It was easier the second time. "I'm in love with your sister."

He let out a sigh. "You know I'm so fucking mad at you."

I shrugged before concluding. "It wasn't meant to happen, Noah."

He stood up and stared down at me. I wasn't sure if he wanted to kill me or breathe fire on me.

"There's only one way to find out what she wants, isn't there?"

I blinked. "What did you say?"

"You fucking heard me, Colton. Now, fuck off."

20

ROSE

"And you're sure you don't mind, sweetie? I would head down to pick it up myself, but..."

I glanced out the window of my Uber while I chatted with Lourde on the phone. "I'm on my way right now. I signed off on the invoices, and I'll have them up to you in a few minutes."

"You're an angel. Feel free to let yourself in when you arrive," Lourde told me before ending the call. The penthouse wasn't far from the restaurant, where I had reservations for dinner before going out with the girls.

I needed a girls' night after the madness of the past month. With five days to the store's opening and everything pretty much in place, it was time to let off some steam.

I touched up my lip gloss before dropping it in my clutch and cringed when I thought about facing Sienna tonight. Even though my heart was broken in two, I had to pretend to be happy, and her brother held the knife that did the damage again.

She'd never get over it if she had the first clue what went down between her brother and me, and there was no point telling her, considering we were as done as an old rerun.

According to Lourde's instructions, I headed straight up to the penthouse with an envelope full of approved invoices for her company's services. Maybe I could ask about Colton and find out what he was up to. The two of them had always been close.

I could've smacked myself for thinking about him. I had to get over the man, end of story. If only I could figure out how.

It didn't register at first, the way acute silence rang out when I stepped out of the elevator. The doors opened straight onto the penthouse, and I was already three strides into the hall leading to the living room before I stopped short, my eyes bulging.

"Surprise." There was Colton, as handsome as ever, holding a glass of champagne. Behind him were his parents and sister, Sienna, my parents, and our families—Uncle Connor and Aunt Pepper, Uncle Magnus and Aunt Evelyn, the boys, Evan included, and the twins, Valentina and Aria.

They lifted their glasses once Connor did. "Congratulations!" Their cheers rang out over my stunned surprise.

"This is for you. Colton set it up." Lourde took the envelope from my hand before I could drop it on the floor. "Celebrate."

I was too overwhelmed to think. Surrounded by people, with Colton in the mix, conflicted between wanting to weep at the sight of him and wanting to ask where he got his nerve. He was acting like nothing had changed and hadn't walked away from me with no explanation.

I wanted to be happy.

I wanted to play along.

"Come on, babe!" Sienna practically shoved her way to

my side and wrapped my fingers around a champagne flute before throwing her arms around me. "Drink up! You deserve it."

"Give her a second," Noah grumbled at my other side. "You don't need to jump on her." Sienna threw him a scowl, one she had on rotation for my brother.

"I was speaking to Rose," she retorted in an overly sweet voice. "Do you mind?" There was venom running under her words, and it raised all kinds of questions, but other issues were more important like the fact that I couldn't breathe.

"I need some air," I announced, touching a hand to my chest. "I wasn't expecting this. I'll be right back." I caught the concerned gazes of my parents and Sienna's surprise as I nudged past them and across the living room, where trays of hors d'oeuvres sat out and numerous bottles of wine and champagne were waiting to be enjoyed.

I was a teenager all over again, having to pretend I wasn't in love with him, that he hadn't broken my heart, putting on a happy face for the sake of my family, and lying through my teeth. I was glad he was in the same room with Noah without them beating each other half to death. How had that come about?

That was a positive development. But it wasn't enough to counter the crushing pressure in my chest by the time I reached the balcony and gripped the stone balustrade, taking deep breaths with my eyes closed. I would have to spend the rest of my life this way. We were always going to be connected by our families.

Over my shoulder, a deep voice murmured, "I wouldn't have planned this if I thought you'd hyperventilate."

Talk about déjù vu. This time, I was the one staring out over the balustrade while Colton crept up behind me. A slight shudder ran through me—anticipation and nerves—

before I stiffened my spine and threw my head back, letting the breeze brush my hair away from my neck. "So it really was you, huh?"

"I might have suggested to my mother that it had been too long since everybody got together, and you deserved to be celebrated. You're about to embark on a new phase in your career. That's a big deal."

I wouldn't insult him by making a wisecrack like I did when this first started weeks ago. No comments about being surprised he took business seriously because I knew how much it meant to him. He had proven himself to me time and again, and I couldn't pretend otherwise. "Thank you."

When he reached the stone railing, I looked his way, reminding myself to breathe. It had been a week since we saw each other, but to my bruised heart, it felt more like years.

I drank in the sight of him. His dark hair—its texture burned into my memory—sharp jaw, broad shoulders, and chiseled profile were so perfect it didn't seem real.

But he was very real, wasn't he? I knew from experience.

"I need to tell you something." He released a sigh before turning my way, jamming his hands into his pockets and almost pleading silently, his dark eyes radiating intensity. "It was a stupid move, walking out on you. I saw those texts and remembered what this was all supposed to be about. I told myself it was for the best. You were going to get what you wanted. I couldn't stand in the way." It came out in a rush like he had to get it out before he lost his nerve.

"You didn't want to leave?" I was almost afraid to believe it.

His lips twitched with a smirk. "Not only because I still think Landon is a waste of bodily organs that could go to someone much more deserving."

I had to stifle a giggle at his creative description. "He is kind of insufferable. You were right about that. I only wanted to see what was on the surface because... I've been burned, and not only by you. I've known too many rich guys to want to bother with them. That was what I told myself."

"What do you tell yourself now?" He inched closer, and my soul screamed with joy.

"I'm telling myself I was stubborn," I admitted. "I was wrong. I should've given you more credit. I shouldn't have made assumptions until I got to know you as an adult."

"Now that you have?" I held my breath when he reached out, stroking my cheek with the back of his fingers. "What would you tell yourself now?"

"I would tell myself I need to be brave enough to admit I fell for you." Now that it was out there, a weight left my shoulders. I was lighter, freer.

"You said it," he whispered, with the beginnings of a smile stirring. "That was brave."

"Thank you. I'm learning." I covered his hand with mine, wrapping my fingers around his. "I would also say I want you with me at the opening. It wouldn't feel right if you weren't there by my side. You made it possible."

"All I did was light a fire under everybody's asses." We shared a soft laugh before his head tipped to the side. "Now that we're on the topic, I've accepted a new job."

"Job?" I had to dial back my surprise in hopes of not insulting him. "Where? What will you be doing?"

"Same as I did with you. My next project is in East Hampton, renovating an old home."

"For your father?" I asked. The night was full of surprises.

"For the family company," he amended, and I understood without being told it was easier for him to think about it that way. The animosity between him and his father wouldn't dissolve overnight. But the fact that he had accepted a position meant they were on their way.

"And is that what you want?" I asked with hope flickering in my heart. "Will it make you happy?"

"No."

That word was a pin in an inflated balloon. "Oh. I'm sorry," I whispered, crestfallen.

"You don't get it." With his other hand, he pulled me in by my waist. "It doesn't matter if the job makes me happy. The only thing that could ever make my life full and complete is you."

Was it really happening?

Was I hearing this?

"You've made me a better man," he told me, his voice tender. "What am I supposed to do without you keeping me in line, calling me on my bullshit, and making life interesting?"

His lips brushed my forehead. I closed my eyes, lost in the magic of the moment—our connection. There was no denying it. It was meant to be.

"You're sure you have it in you to be a one-woman man?" I tipped my head back, searching for the truth in his eyes.

He didn't hesitate. "So long as you're the woman, yes. I have not touched another woman since we started together, and that's the truth. You're all I want. You're all I'll ever need. Please, tell me I'm not alone in this. Otherwise, I think you ruined me."

I touched my fingers to his lips. He didn't need to say another word. My heart knew him well enough already. "I believe you."

"You love me, Rose?" He took my face in his hands, his

touch unbelievably gentle. "Do you? Because I love you from the bottom of my heart."

He went blurry, thanks to the tears that filled my eyes. Happy tears, the happiest I'd ever shed. "Yes. I love you so much. I always have."

Joy radiated from his smile before he pulled me in, lowering his head and kissing me hard. My heart was ready to explode by the time I wrapped my arms around his waist, molding my body to his, clinging to him to stay on my feet once my head started spinning and the world tilted on its axis. He was mine. Finally, after waiting so long and telling myself I was wrong for wanting him, I was in his arms, and he was kissing me for all he was worth, and nothing had ever been more right.

The only thing that could break the moment was the sound of applause coming from inside the penthouse. I knew before we broke the kiss and looked through the glass doors that we had an audience. Our families and friends had watched every moment and now cheered us on. Mom and Lourde cried happy tears, holding onto each other and probably imagining their grandchildren. Even Noah managed to look halfway happy, raising his glass to us with a thin smile.

"Looks like we have their approval," I told Colton, grinning up at him. "That's a pretty good start, right?"

"Are you kidding? Approval from my father? It's a goddamn miracle." He was chuckling as he pulled me close, wrapping his arms around me in a tight hug. "But then again, so are you. I guess I'd better get used to miracles from now on."

21

ROSE

> **Me:** *Coming out tomorrow night?*
> **Sienna:** *Who else will be there?*
> **Me:** *Everybody. Girls and guys. Dinner and drinks.*
> **Sienna:** *I'm not sure. I'll let you know tomorrow.*

Setting my phone aside, I sighed. Sienna swore she was fine with Colton and me, although she hated that I kept it from her and turned away when we showed any kind of PDA. Still, over the past several weeks, she'd used every excuse in the book to avoid getting together if it meant being in a group. The idea of losing my best friend because I found the love of my life was painful. I could only give her space and hope she'd eventually open up and share with me.

The store had been closed for almost an hour. The staff was long gone, having cleaned up after a busy day. There was a profound sense of quiet and peace in the air. I didn't want to move and ruin it.

A sense of pride swelled my heart as I sat in my chair, looking around my cheerful but sophisticated office. It was mine, and I had worked damn hard for it. There was something special about having this space for myself. It wasn't an office in the family's flagship store, something handed down to me. I had seen this through from beginning to end, and a month later, the thrill was still potent.

Still, I couldn't hang around all night. Colton and I had plans for dinner. His work nearby meant continuing to stay in the Hamptons house, giving us all the opportunities in the world to spend every free moment together.

Two months ago, I would never have imagined life turning out this way. Everything had changed so fast and completely that I barely recognized the version of me who believed she had everything figured out and there was no room for surprises. It had taken me a while, but I'd figured out that the unexpected parts of life could be the most rewarding.

Like the man who startled the hell out of me by entering through the back door unannounced. "It's just me," he called out. "Don't come out swinging a broom."

"I only swing a broom at idiots to break up fights," I reminded Colton as he entered the office. He was dressed a little more casually than usual, and somehow, the sight of him in nothing fancier than jeans and a turtleneck left me drooling. Some people managed to make anything look sexy. "Have I kept you waiting?" I asked, eyeing him like he was dessert, and I had a sweet tooth that needed satisfying.

"Technically, no." He joined me behind my desk, swiveling my chair and taking the armrests in his hands to lean down for a lingering kiss. My toes were still curling by the time he added, "It just so happens I couldn't wait to get my hands on you."

"I think you wanted to get me alone here," I ventured,

parting my legs and biting my lip. The spark in his eyes unlocked something feral in me.

"You know..." He glanced around before a deep growl sounded in his throat. "I did tell you we would christen this place one day, didn't I?"

"It's been a whole month since opening," I reminded him while he lowered his head to run his lips over my jaw. "I figured you forgot about that by now."

He pulled his head back far enough that I could see his smirk. "Like I would forget that."

The man was fast. All at once, I was out of my chair, sitting on my desk with his hands at my waist. "What about dinner?" I asked as he attacked my throat, one of his hands sliding over my chest to cup my breast through my silk blouse, my nipple tightening at his touch.

"It'll wait," he growled out close to my ear, scraping his teeth over the lobe until I shivered. "Unless you're in a hurry..."

With both hands, I took hold of his hips and forcefully pulled him in to grind against his hardening dick. "This is all I'm in a hurry for," I whispered against his neck, breathing in his delicious, spicy scent. He rolled his hips, pressing against my already aching clit before claiming my mouth.

Soon, we were lost—kissing, touching, fumbling to get each other out of our clothes. I pushed up on my palms, lifting my ass off the desk so he could pull down my slacks and thong. There was nothing more important than having him inside me.

Now.

"I need you to fuck me," I rasped out between kisses, taking him in my hand once he was free from his boxer briefs and guiding him to where I was wet and beyond ready.

"You like this cock, don't you?" He teased me, probing and pulling back, until I whined my frustration.

"More," I demanded. "*Now*, Colton."

With a grunt, he pushed forward. The mind-blowing friction from his thick cock wiped everything else away. All that existed was this, the point where our bodies joined every time he crashed against me.

"Yes... just like that." I pushed aside a stack of paper to lean back on my hands while each deep stroke shook the desk. Locking my legs around his waist, I worked with him, fucking him as he fucked me, pulling him deeper.

His hands left my hips to slide beneath my blouse, pinching my nipples, adding the electric sensation to everything else already overwhelming my senses—his grunts, his thick shaft stretching me to the limit, the sight of him losing himself in me a little at a time.

"Tell me you love me." I needed to hear it almost as much as I needed more of his cock massaging me inside. As much as I needed his touch and his kiss to push me higher, higher.

His hand cupped the back of my head and pulled me up so his mouth could meet mine in a deep, breathless kiss. "I love you," he whispered, kissing me again. "Always. You're mine." Soon, there was nothing I could do but moan as the tension finally reached its peak.

He joined me, letting go of his control, and by the time he came with a roar, I was quivering around him, gasping and whimpering in the aftermath. There was nothing like the feeling of falling apart in his arms and knowing I was safe.

Or the naughty grin he wore when he looked down at

me. "I'd say we christened your office well. And I think we've earned a big dinner."

Rather than let him go, I locked my legs around his waist. "How about we grab takeout and head straight back to the house instead? As far as I'm concerned, that was only round one."

His grin widened into a knowing smile. "God, I love you."

"I love you."

I had a lifetime of this to look forward to. Colton was mine. Long gone were the delusions of a teenage crush, and in its place was our future. The way it was meant to be.

EPILOGUE
NOAH

Of all fucking days for my CFO to come barging into my office. It wasn't bad enough I'd come in wanting to rip somebody's head off and shit down their throat after losing my second potential listing in as many weeks. I had barely gotten through sloshing whiskey into a glass when he stormed in then made the mistake of eyeing me up. "Don't start with me," I barked out before downing half of the glass. "I've had a hell of a day already, and it isn't noon yet."

"Then you're not going to like what I'm about to tell you." Maxim Forrest was a solid guy with a good head on his shoulders, something that came in handy when it came time to think about numbers and financial decisions. He could also be a real pain in the ass when I was in no fucking mood to hear his sensible bullshit.

"Go ahead. Maybe you'll help me understand how the fuck I just lost another listing." I couldn't breathe. My tie was strangling me, and loosening it didn't seem to help. My throat was tight, and even the welcome burn of the whiskey couldn't distract me from my physical reaction to failure. It wouldn't last forever. That much, I was certain.

It didn't make the situation easier to deal with. "Motherfucker!" The glass shattered against the floor when I spiked it.

I slammed myself into my chair, growling when I remembered the look on that smug bastard's face. "Same as last week. Drake Thomas swooped in and took it out from under me. No explanation, no warning. What the fuck is going on in this city?"

Maxim wasn't blinking, studying me like I was a rare discovery. "You haven't heard? I thought for sure while you were out, you would've heard something."

The hair on the back of my neck lifted in time with a sick feeling that began to spread its way through my gut. "What was I supposed to hear? Get it out fast. I don't feel like playing games."

"Keep in mind, you may be able to pull some strings. Have it silenced by your uncle Connor."

I was liking this less by the second. "Tell me what the fuck you're talking about. What would I need to silence?"

"I'm going to ask you something, and I want your complete honesty. If we're going to get through this, we have to be honest with each other."

"For fuck's sake. I'll be honest with you," I gritted out when he arched an eyebrow. "Whatever you want. Tell me."

"Have you been fucking around with our female clients?"

"Fucking around... as in sleeping with?"

"Is that an attempt at stalling?" I didn't much care for his shitty attitude, right down to the folded arms. "Because a piece is about to be published tomorrow morning. It's due to be syndicated across the country. *Up-and-Coming Real Estate*

Mogul, Son of the Man Behind Farrah Goldsmith Couture, Using His Client List as a Personal Dating Pool and Engaging in Quid Pro Quo Arrangements. You suck my dick, I work harder to sell your property for more money."

It's funny what a person will do when they're caught like a deer in headlights. I didn't know what to expect when Maxim started, but this? It was too ridiculous to believe. I barked out a laugh, equal parts disbelief and disappointment. "That's the best they can do, whoever they are? How fucking juvenile."

"You're telling me it's not true?"

"Seriously? You have to ask me that question? I don't need to troll for pussy. It's a lie. Not even a clever one."

"Let's be honest." He sat in front of the desk, sighing as he settled in. "We've known each other since school. I know how you are. I'm not trying to judge you. It's not like I haven't partied. But you turn it into a sport. So when I hear something like this…"

"Enough," I groaned out. "That would explain why I lost the Park Avenue property."

My head was in a vice, tightening with every breath I took. "Johnny Davies wouldn't want me around his wife if he thinks I'm going to fuck her." Not that I would. Married women weren't my thing, especially the ones who threw themselves at every man they saw.

"There's more," Max added. "Whoever's behind it made up their mind to make you look like a real piece of shit. A nepo baby who couldn't cut it in the family company, so he had to branch out on his own without the skill or work ethic to be a success without using his dick."

"That's bullshit!" I barked. It was one thing to accuse me of using sex to do business, but I drew the line at questioning my motives for opening Goldsmith Real Estate. I wanted something of my own, something I built for myself. I could have easily fallen back on the family's fortune, but it wasn't enough.

"I doubt my uncle could put out anything to counter these accusations. That would look cheesy as fuck," I decided. "Like a kid wetting the bed and blaming the sheets."

"We need to think of something fast, or else what happened today is going to keep happening until we have nothing left." It was rare for him to be that dramatic, which told me he spoke the truth. Normally, he would try to find the silver lining—a positive side to the story.

There was nothing positive about this.

"Short of going door-to-door across Manhattan, how am I supposed to defend myself?" Rubbing my temples, I shrugged. "Do I sue for defamation?"

"I was thinking something a little more immediate, if possible."

"What did you have in mind?" I asked, desperate for ideas.

"Image rehab. We need you to look like a nice guy who's been misunderstood. A hard worker who could have taken the easy way out but instead pulled himself up by his bootstraps or whatever it is old people like to say."

I snickered. "That sounds about right."

"That's how we do it. And you happen to know one of the best PR people in the business, right? Last I heard, anyway."

It took a second for what he was saying to register. "Oh. No. I couldn't use her."

"Why the hell not?" he snapped. "She's good at her job, knows you well, and knows what people respond to. There won't be any of this wasting time getting to know you bullshit, either. She can jump straight in, find what will work best to rehab your image, and we can keep working. That's all that matters now." He jerked a thumb toward the closed door between us and the staff. "You and I will be fine if this goes under. It would be a bitch for the people out there who rely on a paycheck from us."

"You don't need to rub salt in the wound," I muttered, staring at him until he looked away. "I'll call Sienna."

"I'll give you some privacy." In other words, he expected me to get on the phone immediately, leaving me alone to handle convincing Sienna Black into saving my ass.

"I'll be civil in front of our families, but otherwise? I wouldn't piss on you if you were on fire." It had been years since she'd snarled that at me. It was a stupid prank. One I was sure she'd forgotten about. But no. She was determined to hate me for the rest of our lives.

Max had a point, though. She was a star in the PR world, and I needed help immediately—no time for interviews or any of that shit. I reminded myself of that while pulling up her contact and placing a call I knew I'd regret.

She didn't keep me waiting. "Noah Goldsmith." Her voice dripped smug superiority. "Tell me you're not calling for the reason I think."

"You've heard," I stated, already on my way to the bar in the corner. There wasn't enough whiskey in the bottle to combat this.

"I've heard," she confirmed with a snide laugh. "And you're out of your goddamn mind if you think I'd lift a finger to help you get out of your mess."

To be continued...

READ NOAH'S STORY NEXT...

Delicious Tropes you can expect:
Hidden Identity, Forced Proximity and Enemies to Lovers Romance

Preorder SWEET SURRENDER today!

BONUS SCENE

Don't want to let Colton and Rose go just yet?

Grab the FREE bonus scene here:

https://dl.bookfunnel.com/thhergz2kb

ALSO BY MISSY WALKER

ELITE HEIRS OF MANHATTAN SERIES

Seductive Hearts

Sweet Surrender

Sinful Desires

Silent Cravings

Sensual Games

ELITE MEN OF MANHATTAN SERIES

Forbidden Lust*

Forbidden Love*

Lost Love

Missing Love

Guarded Love

Infinite Love Novella

ELITE MAFIA OF NEW YORK SERIES

Cruel Lust*

Stolen Love

Finding Love

SLATER SIBLINGS SERIES

Hungry Heart

Chained Heart

Iron Heart

Small town desires series

Trusting the Rockstar

Trusting the Ex

Trusting the Player

*Forbidden Lust/Love are a duet and to be read in order.

*Cruel Lust is a trilogy and to be read in order

All other books are stand alones.

JOIN MISSY'S BOOK BABES

Hear about exclusive book releases, teasers, discounts and book bundles before anyone else.

Sign up to Missy's newsletter here:
www.authormissywalker.com

Become part of Missy's Facebook Reader Group where we chat all things books, releases and of course fun giveaways!

https://www.facebook.com/groups/missywalkersbookbabes

ACKNOWLEDGMENTS

Big shoutout to my amazing editors who helped whip this thing into shape! Being book one in a new series we really spent a lot of time getting this right. As frustrating as it was, the book is so much better with all the rewrites. Chantell, your eagle eyes and killer feedback totally saved the day.

Huge thanks to my awesome beta readers; Karmin, Maria, Saskia and Ella. Your insights and suggestions really leveled up this manuscript, so a huge thank you.

To all the fans out there, you're the real MVPs! Your love for The Elite Men has made this series a possibility. I can't thank you enough for your endless support and messages you send through. I check every single one of them x

And to my fam, thanks for putting up with all those late nights and crazy deadlines. Couldn't have done it without you!

Much love,
Missy x

ABOUT THE AUTHOR

Missy is an Australian author who writes kissing books with equal parts angst and steam. Stories about billionaires, forbidden romance, and second chances roll around in her mind probably more than they ought to.

When she's not writing, she's taking care of her two daughters and doting husband and conjuring up her next saucy plot.

Inspired by the acreage she lives on, Missy regularly distracts herself by visiting her orchard, baking naughty but delicious foods, and socialising with her girl squad.

Then there's her overweight cat—Charlie, chickens, and border collie dog—Benji if she needed another excuse to pass the time.

If you like Missy Walker's books, consider leaving a review and following her here:

instagram.com/missywalkerauthor
facebook.com/AuthorMissyWalker
tiktok.com/@authormissywalker
amazon.com.au/Missy-Walker
bookbub.com/profile/missy-walker

Made in the USA
Coppell, TX
25 November 2025